T0162631

A DIFFERENCE A DAY MAKES

Order this book online at www.trafford.com
or email orders@trafford.com

Most Trafford titles are also available at major online book retailers.

Printed in the United States of America.

ISBN: 978-1-4669-6167-8 (sc)
ISBN: 978-1-4669-6166-1 (hc)
ISBN: 978-1-4669-6168-5 (e)

Library of Congress Control Number: 2012918271

Trafford rev. 11/09/2012

www.trafford.com

North America & international
toll-free: 1 888 232 4444 (USA & Canada)
phone: 250 383 6864 ♦ fax: 812 355 4082

Tonya sat in the car waiting for Mr. Jones for a few minutes as she looked around the parking lot.

A tall gentleman really nice looking in his late thirties or early forties, nicely dressed in a navy blue suit came out of the laundry facility, did not look like a person doing laundry she thought to herself

Maybe he owns the place.

As he approached my car I thought to myself this must be Mr. Jones not a bad looking brother.

Excuse me are you Tonya?

Yes I am.

I'm Walter Jones. Nice to meet you Mr. Jones I said as I extended my hand as I got out of my car.

How are you?

Very well thank you; Mr. Jones said.

Well I have three listing for you to see. The first one is not to far from here.

Let me get my car Mr. Jones said and I'll follow you or you can ride with me if you want he said.

No thank you Ill drive my car I have all my things I use to work in here

I lead, you follow I said with a big smile on my face.

You're the boss he said.

The first address is 1921 W 76th street a two bedroom two bathroom home in this nice neighborhood with older residents.

It took us less than ten minutes to get to the property.

We pulled up the house has a great curb appeal freshly painted white with blue trim manly I thought to myself.

I parked in the driveway, Mr. Jones parked in front of the house at the curb.

I took the paper work and open the car door and stepped out stood by my car and waited for Mr. Jones

We walked up to the front and I unlocked the lock box that held the door keys and open the door to the house.

In the entry of the house was brown tile flooring and to the left the liven room with matching brown carpet, we walked through the liven room and around a wall to the kitchen.

The kitchen was small and dark the floor has black and white square sticky tile. The cabinets are dark brown just a little dark for my taste I thought to myself; what do you think Mr. Jones?

It okay to me so far.

The bedrooms are through this way; we walked through the kitchen down a small hallway to the first bedroom, which is the master bedroom with a bathroom off to the side

The bathroom was a nice size with a tub and a shower double sink and a separate room with a door for the toilet area this was nice. This was a very nice room with lot of windows and a large closet.

At the other end of the hallway was the second bedroom.

We walked down the hall to the room I could feel Mr. Jones looking at me as I walked in front of him.

Ms Tonya, can I ask you something personal?

Sure. I said.

Does your husband like you doing a job like this?

A job like this?

What do you mean?

Showing vacant houses to strangers.

I'm not married, Mr. Jones.

I would have lied if I had been wearing a ring on at least one of my fingers.

Oh! I see he said with a funny grin on his face.

Mr. Jones, will the home you pick be for you and your family? I asked.

No I'm single, he said

As we finished the tour of the first home I started to wonder about this guy.

Mr. Jones and I finished looking at the other room, bathroom back yard and the front yard.

This is okay he said but not with to much enthusiasm let just see what the next property looks like, so I went to lock up the keys so we could leave and go to the next property. We returned to our cars and headed to the next house.

At the office Kenny ran into Ray another lawyer friend of his.

What's up stranger?

Hay! Long time no see, so how is California treating you he asked playfully.

Cool Kenny said.

Ray shook Kenny hand.

What's been up here man? Kenny asked.

The same shit different day.

I know that's right man.

What bring you to town Ray asked curiously?

This time I'm getting the rest of my things and moving them to my new office in L.A.

The movers will be in later to pick the last of my boxes and Fed X them to me.

Man that's cool I wish you the best we'll miss you dude.

Same here Kenny said as he shook Ray's hand.

Well good seeing you, I'm off to court Ray said lightly.

Good luck man. Kenny said as he walked to his office.

Kenny sat at his desk and open the top drawer and started removing the things in it.

After a few minutes His mind was not into packing all he could think of was Christina

How she tasted to him and how her body moved under him when he made love to her last night.

Man she could return move for move damm that was good he thought to himself.

I have to get this office packed up so I can get out of here Kenny said as he rubbed his hand over his face to regroup and clear his thoughts.

This woman is driving me wild I have to get a grip.

He thought to himself as he lifted his top lip to his nose hoping he could still smell the sent of her sweet juices.

Mr. Mathews you have a call on line one the voice of his receptionist said over the intercom on his phone it's Ms. Williams.

Thank you Kenny said trying not to sound to excited.

Before Kenny answered the phone he got up and went around his desk to close the door to his office.

Good morning sweetheart, Kenny said as he put the phone to his ear.

His voice made Christina inside tighten up.

Her hot spot began to get wet all over again.

Good morning Christina said, thank you for a wonderful night.

I called to see if you were feeling as good as I do?

Baby I was just thinking of you Kenny said, as he felt a rise in his pants.

Oh yeah, Christina said, smiling because she worked his ass good.

I needed that work out she thought because she had not been to the gym in two days with all the last minute work and packing for this trip.

I hope I wasn't to wild she thought, but I haven't had sex in so long I needed that she thought.

Baby the reason I called is that I need to go to the store but I don't know where it is.

Yeah! Right I needed to here your voice she said to herself

Do you need me to pick up some thing on my way back sweetie, Kenny asked?

No baby.

Is there a store in walking distance?

I felt like cooking and what I need is not here, but it's all right.

No I don't want you board; Kenny said.

I'm okay baby, Christina said as she rubbed her sore legs.

If you want to go my other car is in the garage and the keys are in the kitchen drawer.

The market is five blocks away if you go left out of the driveway to the first corner make a right and go down five blocks you will see the market okay.

Okay Christina said.

There is some money in the nightstand in my bedroom.

I have enough I'll see you when you get here.

Christina I'll be there in a couple of hours, Kenny said.

I miss you already, I miss you to Christina said.

Kenny returned home to a smell that was not something he expected, Christina had the whole house smelling good.

Baby what have you been doing? Don't you know your on vacation?

Hi to you to Christina said as she walked up and kissed Kenny on his lips.

Baby this is great a home cooked meal in my own house this is a first.

Kenny put his brief case on the floor in the entry way and put his arms around Christina waist and lifted her up and kissed her with a hungry, sexy, passionate and long kiss that he had long for the whole time he was away from here.

Christina reached up and placed her hands around his neck and accepted the kiss and returned it back.

Kenny's kisses would melt chocolate that just came out of the freezer they where just that hot to her.

Kenny and Christina stopped because things were starting to happen Kenny's dark bar

Starting to grow in his pants and Christina felt it pushing up against her as he held her up.

She wanted to wrap her legs around him and let him do what ever he wanted to do.

Christina felt wetness beginning to form in her hot spot.

Kenny baby, Christina said, baby we need to eat last night we missed dinner.

All right but you know you were saved by the dinner bell. Kenny said as he placed Christina to her feet.

Everything looks nice and smells so good.

Thank you.

After seeing the last house Tonya felt a little funny about Mr. Jones it was the way he had watched her through the last house he did not seem interested in it at all.

Mr. Jones this the last house on my list today and what do you think of it.

Well it's nice and all but the other one we just left suite me better, do you mind showing me the last bedroom again? The one in the back please.

Sure, Tonya felt nervous about that request.

Just as Tonya turn to lead Mr. Jones down the hallway to the back bedroom she felt Mr. Jones grabbed her by the arm and slammed her body into the wall and put his hand over her mouth to keep her from screaming.

She try hard to make a loud noise thinking that would make him scared and let her go.

As he pulled her down the hall way she kick and kicked but felt helpless.

She kept kicking, one of her shoes fell off but she kept kicking.

Mr. Jones had her by the neck chocking her with one hand the other over her mouth from behind what was he going to do to me? Tonya tried to fight grabbing his suit jacket trying to scratch his arms trying to make him release her.

Stop fighting bitch.

PUNCH, PUNCH, PUNCH.

Stop fighting, Oh you're a bad ass, Stop fighting he said as he chock her tighter and tighter

Tonya fell too the ground.

After dinner Christina and Kenny went into town, Kenny had planed to take Christina to a movie but instead they just walked around and took in the sight of New York it felt good just to be out and in good company.

Are you okay? Kenny asked?

Yes this is real nice just to get out and walk I don't do enough of this.

I promise things are going to be different when I get back. Christina said I enjoy this I needed this time out period.

Thank you for the invite. Christina said.

No Thank you for agreeing to come with me.

Christina and Kenny held hands and walked looking around and enjoying the time together before the chill of the New York air sent them back home.

After arriving back Kenny and Christina went in the kitchen to get a hot cup of coffee

Kenny went over to the coffee pot and got the empty coffee pot and took it over to the sink.

Christina got the bag of fresh coffee beans out of the cabinet and placed it on the counter.

Kenny reached up in the top cabinet to get the grinder to grind the coffee beans for the coffee.

I really like this coffee Christina said.

I got this from Jamaica.

Beep, Beep, Beep, Beep.

What is that? Kenny asked.

It sound like a phone Christina said.

Kenny and Christina followed the sound as they walked out of the kitchen and down the hallway towards the bedrooms.

Beep, Beep, Beep, Beep.

It's coming from your bags sweetheart.

I think it's my cell phone, I thought I turned it off.

Christina reached into her Gucci bag that match her two suitcases that was still not un packed yet.

Here it is I guess I didn't turn it off she said as she looked over in Kenny's direction.

Two messages that strange I hope the hospital haven't gone up in smoke.

Christina flipped the phone open and pushed the button to access her messages.

Christina sweetie this is mother Gardener have you talked to Tonya? If you can reach her tell her to call me ok, I haven't been able to reach her all day.

Thank you baby.

Christina looked surprised, is everything okay baby? Kenny asked after he saw the look on her face.

Message 2 she heard her cell phone said.

Christina this is Milo I'm looking for my sis she was supposed to come by mom's pad but she's a no show I thought you two were together. That's if you're back from out of town we talked yesterday and she said you were out of town.

I thought maybe you were back and you two might be together get back with me.

I'm out.

That's weird.

What's that baby?

Tonya you remember.

Yes.

That was her mother and her brother they're looking for Tonya.

So they're calling you?

Yeah.

That's a first, I wonder where she is; she's not with me.

I'll call them and let them know.

Tonya went missing for two days until Jeff came back to the office.

Has anyone heard from Tonya?

Everyone in the office said no.

Jimmy the last man in the row of cubical where Tonya sits said she was in two days ago and she went to meet a client she left you the info on your desk.

Oh, I just thought she had been in the office already and I missed her.

No, Jimmy said she was not here yesterday either.

That was weird Tonya always checked into the office, something was not right.

Jeff looked on his desk to find the information and sat down to call Tonya.

Kenny felt himself sweating as it got hot in the room Christina legs were wrapped around him as he gripped her by her waist and thrust long and deep inside her as she moaned with pleasure oh yes! Oh baby you feel so good she said.

His body felt good to the touch as she rubbed up his back as he took control of each movement don't stop she said oh don't stop.

The sweat dripped off his face on to her face.

With one hand Christina wiped his face as she watches him enjoy what he was getting.

The heat was intense between them Kenny looked down and stared at Christina face beautiful he said as he continue to slip in and out of her walls of warm fluid.

Baby damm your wet baby, Kenny said, I like that.

You make me like that Christina said.

Damm girl that's all Kenny could say.

Early the next morning Christina call Mrs Gardner back.

Hi Mother Gardener this is Christina.

Christina how are you? Have you heard from Tonya?

No. That's why I was calling I spoke with her two days ago I'm in New York.

Oh! Baby I didn't know that. Well I guess I'll try her house one more time and then I'll call the office again.

Okay feel free to call my cell again if you don't fine her and I tell you what I will make some phone calls and see if any of the other girls heard from her.

Christina hung up the phone and looked at Kenny.

Ring, Ring, Ring, Ring.

The mobile customer you're trying to reach at this number is unavailable leave a message at the beep.

Sorry the mailbox of the mobile customer is full please try again.

Man Jeff said her cell phone is full and she not answering, I'll call her mother house to see if she left town.

Just as he picks up the phone it rang. Hello.

Hello I'm trying to reach the real estate office.

Excuse me this is the real estate office please forgive me, how can I help you?

I'm calling to speak with Tonya please.

Is it anything that I can help you with?

No. This is her mother, is she in today.

This is Jeff her partner I was just looking up your number to call you.

Why, fear was in her voice.

No one in the office has seen or heard from her. For the last two days I've been trying to find your number to call and ask if she had left town or something.

I don't think so not with out calling and letting some one know.

I think I'll call the police her mother said.

Milo Tonya Mother called out in the house.

Yes, Mother I called your sister job and no one has seen her in two days they said.

Mom I'm getting dress call the police I'll call dad at his office and get him home.

Christina called Jackie, Angie, Lisa, and Bridgett no one has heard from her.

Baby I'm starting to get scared, Christina said.

Kenny walked over to her and rapped his arm around her, baby she'll be fine.

Christina maybe she with that guy she met at the club.

Lets get something to eat and we can call the airport and go back to L.A if you're that worried.

I think her mom would call if she not okay. We'll stay and finish up here.

Christina and Kenny ordered a bottle of red wine, and took their menus and looked them over.

This night was beginning to feel strange, what's up baby? Kenny asked you seem to be in another place right now.

I'm sorry every since the call from Tonya mom I just think now something is up. She never leave town and not tell me.

Kenny could see sadness in Christina eyes.

I know that Milo is in town and you can't pull them two apart when he's in town she even stood him up she has never done anything like that she and her brother is very close plus her brother has been gone for the past two years.

Let's say we order and eat and if her mom doesn't call back we'll call them when we get back to the house Kenny said.

Okay.

The waitress returned with the wine, Kenny took a sip of the wine and savored it.

So how do you like this vacation? Kenny asked to lighten up the mood.

I'm enjoying it and my host very much, Thank you.

Christina begin to relax, and thought to herself if I don't get a call she was sure to call as soon as she hit the door.

As she watch Kenny from across the table she could see this man was truly a dream come true. The compassion, tenderness and patients he shows were rare in men these days.

Everyman these days are out for themselves.

Kenny's full lip makes me just want to kiss him and not stop for air. The whole ambiance of this place with the dimly lit tables and the warm sandy colors that were on the wall and the low jazz that played in the back was doing something to Christina head she wanted to pass up dinner and go home and have some more desert she said to herself stop thinking so bad relax you got him.

The more she looked the more she wanted, she was glad that Kenny helped her to live, care, and feel again, especially feel again life was really boring until Mr. Mathews came along.

Is this the relative of Tonya Gardener? The voice on the phone asked.

Yes it is this is her mother who is this?

Mrs. Gardener felt her heart begin to beat fast inside of her chest sweat began to bead up on her forehead.

The back ground in the phone let her know that the call was coming from a hospital she could here an intercom or something real loud calling someone's name.

She felt her legs began to shake; she looked over at the chair that was near the table where she stood on the phone.

Who is this she begin to scream into the phone she felt herself get real scared no one ever called here looking for Tonya gardener mother since she was in the third grade attending 116th Street school and she and Christina got in trouble throwing wet tissue up in the girl's bathroom and making it stick to the ceiling.

This is Detective Frank Dent, with the Los Angeles Police dept.

I'm calling about your daughter.

Tonya mother started screaming JESUS! JESUS! JESUS.

Mom! What's wrong?

Milo came running into the liven room.

Mom what's wrong!

Milo ran to his mother side and took the phone from her hand and sat her in the chair.

Hello! Hello! This Milo Gardener.

Mr. Gardener this is detective Dent we have a young lady her at Daniel freeman Hospital

And her ID said that her name is Tonya Gardener.

I know there is a missing person out on your daughter Tonya Gardener, and this is the number on the missing person report.

I was wondering if you are someone in your family could come down here. I'll come down there I'm Tonya's brother.

I was the one who got the missing person report, the young lady we—

Man I'm Tonya brother is my sister all right! Milo shouted into the phone.

The person we have down her is very badly beaten, and the ID that was found on this person has your sister information on it I'm not sure who this person is or if she will survive through the night the detective said.

What the fuck! Are you saying man! Milo shouted than remember that his mother was right there.

The young lady is barely recognizable.

I'll be right there.

Mr. Gardener please comes to the intensive care unit.

Click. Milo hung up the phone.

Milo pasted back and forth before he said anything to his mother tears was falling from his eyes, his fists were in balls, He was trying to clam himself down.

Mom, Milo said in a whisper I think they found Tonya.

The man said that the person was badly beaten and they need someone to come and ID this woman.

Mom did you here me? Mrs. Gardener sat there staring into space rocking back and forth trying to keep it together.

Mom, their not sure who this person is so keep it together mom please.

I'll go, you stay until I call you, you call dad and get him home just in case

Mom, call him now. Milo said as he turned to walk to the front door.

Milo reached for his mom and hugged her real tight and kisses her head like she was his child instead of the other way around.

At the red light Milo prayed Dear god its me Milo I need you right now and Lord I know you already know what I want to ask you so here I go. Father please let this person be an over comer if this is Tonya Lord help this family.

Lord give us strength lord to see thing through your eyes I know your word said father that you will never leave us and Lord please stand close to us now in this situation don't let this be my sister to the only God our savior be glory, majesty, power and authority, through Jesus Christ our lord, now and forever more! Amen.

Mrs. Gardener kids grew up in a Christian church and they know on whom to call on.

Milo finishes praying; he could see the Hospital a block away.

Milo entered the parking lot of the hospital and parked in the emergency room parking space.

Just as he entered the emergency room lobby he felt his stomach knot up.

Damm he said to himself.

Milo looked around and he could see the emergency room was full of sick people waiting to see a doctor.

I hate this place he said to himself.

Children crying and parents with tired looks on their faces sat waiting for their names to be called.

The hospital was a place Milo hated to be in; when he turns to the left he spotted a sign that said information desk.

That it he thought to himself I'll ask the young lady sitting at this desk where the intensive care unit is.

Hello Milo said to the girl at the desk, Hi she said.

Oh! Hi. She said again after she looked up from the newspaper she was looking at.

Boy you are fine she thought to herself as her face expression lit up.

Milo always got that reaction from woman, if this was any other day he would have been flattered.

Milo new he was a nice looking man it's been told to him most of his life.

Milo started building his body back in high school after he join the football team and the worked paid off.

He stands over six feet heavily muscled and so fine that he looks like a buff model.

Milo never had a problem meeting women as a of matter fact he had women in every area code where he did business he traveled extensively for his business.

These women were attractive to his looks and body, being in construction keeps him in great shape.

The women Milo enjoy dating are all beautiful women, models, businesswomen; even his Dentist has dated him.

Milo has always been a hit it and quit it type of guy because he is the owner of three construction companies and with his businesses he's never stayed in a town long enough to settle down with no one women business was first and he took great pride in his accomplishments.

Can you tell me where the intensive care unit is?

Who are you her to see?

Detective Dent.

Oh, she said.

You can take the elevators over there to your right to the third floor exit and turn right.

Thank you.

Milo went to the elevator and pushes the up button and the doors opened after entering the elevator his stomach was really starting to hurt and the hospital smell was making him feel really nervous.

The doors open at the third floor Milo stepped out just as nurse was passing Milo grabbed her arm can you tell me where detective Dent is?

Shocked the nurse pointed to the nurse station across the hall where a tall gentleman was standing. There he is right there she said.

The nurse could tell that Milo didn't mean any harm by grabbing her and he was in a big hurry so she shook it off then she looked over at another nurse standing their with raised eyebrows with wow did you see him look on their faces, shit fine as he is he could grab her arm any time she thought.

Detective Dent I'm Milo Gardener.

Hello Mr. Gardener nice to meet you he said as they shook hands.

The situation is, let's talk in here detective Dent said after he look over to the room across from them after he notice that all the nurses at the nurse station was looking and listening.

What we have is a black female that fits the description your family left at the station.

This woman face has been badly beat and it's hard for me to tell if she's Ms. Gardener.

I appreciate your help on this detective Dent said.

If this is not your sister please forgive me for the call.

Where is she? Milo asked with excitement in his voice he needed to get this over because he was feeling sicker by the minute.

Follow me this way detective Dent said

Christina didn't get any messages from the girls about Tonya.

Kenny I think I'll call Tonya's mom to see if any thing new has come up.

Okay Kenny said as he took her hand and led her to the kitchen to fix them a drink.

Christina reached for the cordless phone on the counter and dial the number.

Ring. Ring. Hello this is Mr. Gardener he said with his professional manner.

Hi, this is Christina pop.

Hi sweetheart, Christina always call Mr. Gardener pop just like his kids did.

How are you? Have Tonya call yet?

Baby not yet we did get a call form a detective earlier about a woman they found.

What! Christina yelled into the phone was this woman dead?

Tears came to her eyes.

No baby she was beaten very badly but they can't tell who she is.

Milo went over to the hospital to check it out I was just waiting for the call as we speak.

Where are you Mr. Gardener asked?

I'm in New York I've been her for three days but I'm on the next flight out you can bet that pops.

Baby we'll call you if we here anything.

Mom and I will call everyone as soon as we know something he said with sadness in his voice.

No pop I'm on my way Christina said.

Mr. Gardener was a strong man with a good heart to here him sound so down made Christina just want to cry.

He worship the ground his family walked on he could not have been a prouder man.

Pops I'm on my way I'll be on the next flight and I'll call you all when I get back in town tell mom I'll make some more calls and I'll see you later.

Oh! My god.

Christina began to cry something is wrong, Kenny I can feel it.

What's the matter? Kenny said as he walked back into the kitchen.

Christina was sitting on the floor next to the cabinets she was already off the phone.

Christina was crying, I need a flight out of here tonight right now she yelled.

Kenny rushed over to where she was sitting what happen?

It's Tonya she's still missing and a detective called the house and had her brother come to the hospital.

The hospital why? They found a woman badly beaten in a house and she fit the description pops left at the police station but they were not for sure.

I just want to get back to LA. Now.

After making a few calls Kenny had two flights back to LA that was leaving in two hours.

Christina was packed and waiting for the car to arrive at the house to take them to the airport.

Kenny was finishing up a few things in his home office when he heard the horn beep.

Baby he heard Christina say, He felt sad that they had to leave so early but he new this was important to Christina.

Baby the car is here.

I'm right here Kenny said as he put his arms around her waist calm down sweetheart we'll be there in no time I promise.

Christina wrapped her arms around his neck and she kissed him, I'm sorry our trip was interrupted you don't have to leave with me I know you still have things to do.

It's all right baby your first in my life right now Kenny replied as he bent down to kiss her again.

That made her feel so good, but her heart was still sad and she was stilled worried.

Ring the sound of the doorbell broke the heated kiss.

Kenny reached and opens the door.

Mr. Mathews I'm Henry I'll be taking you to the airport.

Kenny reached over and picked up his and Christina bags and handed then to Henry.

Is that all sir Henry asked with respect.

Yes Kenny said in a hurry I'll see you at the car Henry said as he turned to walk away.

While at the airport Christina made a few more phone calls.

Kenny made a call to his office to tell them that the rest of his things are to be sent to the LA office and to rush the box on his desk next day service.

Christina decided to call the hospital, she called over to her office and Kim answered.

Hey Kim this is Christina I need a favor.

How is the vacation going? Are you enjoying yourself she asked with excitement in her voice?

I'm on my way back.

What? Kim said in disbelieve

You know Tonya she is missing and I think a woman was brought in to the hospital this morning. Kim could here Christina was sad her voice was soft and shaky.

You are kidding Christina; Kim said with sadness in her voice, what you need me to do.

Listen Christina said I need you to go fine out where this person is and check if that's Tonya.

How did you here about the person that came in?

Tonya mom had called me a day ago looking for Tonya because she has not been heard from.

I called and her dad said a Detective called and said that a woman was found and brought over there.

What? This is crazy.

I'll call and see who came in, in the last few hours and I'll check it out and call you.

Where are you?

I'm at the airport in New York now but I'll be in route to LA in the next Fifteen minutes.

Please do this for me and let me know something as soon as possible.

Sure Kim said.

Kim started phoning some departments in the hospital first she started with the Emergency room.

Emergency Jackie speaking how can I help you?

Jackie this is Kim in Children ward west.

What's up?

Hay check and see if a woman name Tonya Gardener got admitted in through there this morning?

Let see Jackie said as she pick up a clipboard with all the morning admits.

I don't see that name.

What about last night?

No not a single person with that name.

Matter of fact no woman was admitted last night.

Girl there was a woman who was found in an empty house this morning she was beaten so bad that no one knows who she is.

The police has been here all morning hoping that she wake up.

What do she look like?

I walked over to the patient area this morning when she was brought in. All I know that she is a black woman in her early thirties.

I need to come down and see.

Why? Jackie asked.

Because Ms Williams friend is missing she never leave town without telling her family and her parents are worried.

How old is she? I

I think she is Thirty or late Twenty's.

Well the lady is in the intensive care unit with a detective watching her.

I'll come see. Tonya is a Realtor and she could have been showing that empty house to a client Kim thought to herself.

I hope this is not her. My God Christina will be crushed if it's her.

Milo followed detective Dent into a empty waiting room and sat across from him.

I need you to understand that the woman face is really beat bad and it is swollen she has tubs coming from her mouth and she in a coma.

Are you ready?

Yeah man I need to see if this is my sister I hope it's not Milo thought to himself.

Milo stood up and followed detective Dent into the room across from them with the curtains closed.

In the room Milo could see a fragile little figure under the hospital blanket lying in the bed in the middle of the room with machines every where.

Milo heard the machine working to keep this woman alive IV tubes, breathing machine, oxygen canisters, and a crash cart was in the room two chairs were in the corner of the room and a table next to the window.

The sun came through the window and made the room look as if the lights were on, you can here traffic out side the day was bright and cheerful the trees were in full color but for Milo he was having a very dark day.

Milo walked over to the bed, but every step felt like he had cement on the bottom of his shoes his step was slow and weighted.

Mr. Gardener are you all right? Detective Dent asked?

Milo spotted a scar on the right side of Tonya face that was familiar to him because he was the cause of that scar.

When they were young Milo and Tonya were bike riding Tonya was scared to ride close to the park cars.

Milo know this so he rode up fast and close to her while they were riding in the street Tonya moved close to a park car just as a man open his door.

Tony hit the door and flew off her bike and hit her face on the pavement. Leaving a deep wound in her face

This was a big thing the ambulance came Ms Gardener was called to the seen.

Milo was all shaken up Tonya was on the ground bleeding.

Milo road in the ambulance with Tonya he kept telling her how sorry he was and he was just playing.

Tonya was crying and she would not talk to him, Milo knew his mother was going to punish him after all this was over.

Milo did not like the feel of the cold Hospital all the people there were hurt. He came through the Emergency department with the ambulance workers.

Mrs. Gardener followed the Ambulance. Milo didn't want to leave his sister side.

People were screaming in the room next to Tonya's room that made him scared.

Tonya got ten stiches in her face and they left.

Milo regretted that day he and Tonya became closer after that.

Milo quickly turn his head to the detective this is my sister.

Mr. Gardener your sure?

Yes. Milo shouted yes. Who did this he yelled that mutherfucker is dead, dead I promise you that.

Tonya Milo said, as he held her hand in his.

Tonya I'm here Tonya I'm sorry.

Mr. Gardener—Milo you can call me Milo he said.

I have to call my mother and father to let them know.

Calm down Milo, Detective Dent said with a calm manner

Tonya I'm here mom will be here soon he said as he bent down and kissed her head.

Kim went down to the intensive care unit to inquire about the woman that was brought in.

As she exited the elevator she ran into her friend Shelia.

Shelia has worked this unit for ten years and she run the department.

Hey you Kim said as she stepped out of the elevator.

What are you doing up here?

I heard about a woman that was brought in this morning.

Oh! Yea she's messed up bad.

My boss best friend is missing-

Christina friend Tonya, I know Tonya.

Shelia said.

Well she asked me to check any new admitting to see if she has come in here.

I haven't seen the person but she is on this floor I'm just getting in.

Can we check? Kim asked.

Yes all I know is that we have a badly beaten Jane Doe.

Let's go check Shelia said.

Kim and Shelia walked over to the nurse's station and ran into detective Dent.

Shelia this is detective dent a nurse at the station said.

Detective she said as she extended her hand. I'm Shelia Smith head nurse on this floor I here we have a Jane Doe.

Well as of a minute age, we did. Now I have the identity of this woman she's a Realtor form Riverside Reality, Her name is Tonya Gardener.

Her family had a missing person out on her, it was the only one we had so I called the family when she was found and the brother just identified her.

He's right there he said as he pointed to the man on the pay phone down the hall.

Shelia ran into the room and started crying.

Kim ran in after her they were both crying Tonya I'm so sorry Kim said.

Tonya lied there still as they gathered around her bedside. Shelia came out of the room in tears.

Shelia gathered all the nurses together around the nurses station and informed them that this is a friend and she wanted to be informed at all times of her condition.

Kim came out into the hallway and headed for the nurse station to call Christina.

Christina cell phone rang just as she and Kenny exited the baggage claim at the Airport.

Christina looked at the cell phone and the caller ID displayed unknown caller.

Who could this be she thought. Hello, Hey Christina it's me Kim.

Christina could feel Kim was not in a happy mood and that something was really wrong.

Kim what's the matter? Is every thing all right?

Christina it's Tonya she been found and I'm sorry to tell you this she's here.

Kim was crying she's here.

Kim what are you saying tell me Christina yelled in the phone every one in baggage claim got quiet.

Kenny stood there looking at Christina he know the news was not good news.

Just as he turn to put the luggage down on the curb a black Limo pulled up.

Mr. Mathews the driver said as he got out of the car put these in the back Kenny said as he walked back over to where Christina was standing

Baby come on the car is here.

Baby what's the matter?

Kim calm down he heard her say.

Kim tell me what happen I'm here in LA I'm on my way to the Hospital.

Tonya she's her in ICU she was beaten bad she's in a coma her parents are on the way.

How do they know it's her?

Tonya brother is here and he identified her.

Wait what do you mean he identified her? Is she dead?

No, but she is in grave condition Kim said through her tears.

Christina screamed and screamed Kenny caught her just as she was about to fall to the ground.

Help me put her in the car he said to the driver with anger in his voice.

Baby what happen? Oh baby it's all right Kenny wrapped her in his strong arms Christina cried as she laid her head on his tight big chest that made her feel safe.

Please hurry Kenny yelled to the driver from the back of the Limo.

Take us to Daniel Freeman Hospital

Yes sir the driver said with a hurry tone

Tonya mother and father arrived at the Hospital and was meet by the Detective in the lobby.

Mr. And Mrs. Gardener I'm Detective Dent can you follow me please.

No Mr. Gardener said in a very rude way I need to see my daughter. Where is she?

Mr. Gardener I will take you to her in a minute.

Please follow me I need to inform you of what happen.

Please lord help us Mrs. Gardener said please Jesus.

Folks come with me and have a seat in here.

Is my daughter all right?

How bad is she?

Where did you find her?

Where is she? Mrs. Gardener shot questions at Detective Dent fifty miles an hour.

Christina and Kenny came through the entrance of the Hospital and headed for the elevator.

On the elevator there was a young man standing in the right corner with dry tears on his face trying not to make eye contact with any one.

Christina and Kenny stepped in and push the button and the door shut.

Kenny stepped behind Christina and wrapped his arms around her waist.

Baby he said as she laid her head back against his powerful chest.

Yes, she said.

It's going to be all right.

I'm scared baby Christina said with sadness showing in her pretty face.

Tonya was lying very still, her brother was by her side so was Kim and one of the nurses from the nurse station; she was checking the IV drip machine.

Milo keep saying Jesus your word is right.

Jesus your word say you will never leave nor forsake us please Jesus here my cry send your Angels to camp around my sis and make her better please father I pray and turn this over to you right now in the name of Jesus.

Christina entered the room, the room was bright and the little shape that she seen from the doorway could not be Tonya.

Milo spotted her and got up to greet her.

Milo embraced Christina and they cried.

Milo no she said this is not Tonya.

Yes sis it is. I'm sorry Milo said.

What happen?

I don't know.

Christina walked over to the bed and prayed.

Prayer changes all things she always said that.

Milo noticed Kenny standing in the doorway, Hay man what's up? He said as he wiped the tears from his eyes.

Hay I'm Kenny Christina friend.

Oh! Cool man come in.

Christina held Tonya hand shaking her head as the tears ran down her face, who on earth could have been so mean?

Tonya if you can here me baby it's me Christina I'm here baby.

Please get better we love you baby.

Mr. And Mrs. Gardener walked in the room. The detective filled them in on what they think happen to their daughter and what to expect when they went up to her room.

Mrs. Gardener came in slow with her hand over her mouth eyes wide open and shacking.

Mom Milo said as he ran just before she fainted in his arms.

Mr. Gardener stared at his baby girl lying there barely alive.

I'll kill that motherfucker he said when I get my hands on that motherfucker dear god help me.

Dad, Milo said calm down.

Milo sat his mother in the chair near the window with the help of a Kenny.

Dad I've made some calls and this will be handled.

What do you mean Mr. Gardener said with fear in his voice?

Don't worry about it.

Mr. Gardner knew that Milo was the younger version of himself and when you mess with his family you have crossed the wrong line.

Son don't be crazy the detective will find this person.

I hope that he don't I just need a few minutes with him first.

Milo eyes told every one in the room that he meant business.

Detective Dent went back to his office to study all the papers that had come in on the day Christina Gardener was last seen.

Christina spent the next few weeks working long hours and spending all of her lunch breaks visiting Tonya.

Four weeks had passed and Tonya was still in a coma most of the swelling in her face had gone down and you could tell it was Tonya.

Her mother came every day from 6:00am till 9:00pm.

Her father worked and came to see her after work; he had taken Two weeks of his vacation and spent every waking hour at the hospital.

Milo and a few of his cousins and boys spent the last few weeks doing street research

They had found out through the grape vine that there was a guy that fit the description in the neighbor hood about two weeks ago.

He hung out in the laundry matt on Normandie most days. He come around like he is the owner from what the guys came up with.

Kenny went back to New York Three time to close the deal on his property and move his life to Los Angeles.

Four weeks ago Christina thought life was looking good; I met the love of my life.

Tonya was at the high light of her business selling homes by the dozen driven a brand new car and life was good.

Now what the hell happen? A difference a day makes.

The phone rang breaking her thoughts, hello.

Hay girl how are you?

Rhonda is a friend of Tonya and Christina and she heard about Tonya thought some other friends of theirs.

Rhonda went to college with them and later moved to St Louis to become a Doctor.

There's no news Christina said.

Well Tonya is in Gods hand and we know that he loves us and he'll make a way.

Girl we were just on top of the world.

Shit just starting going crazy, I can't believe the crap that's happening.

Young ass Koby Bryant in the news with this rape shit who knows what happen but him and her.

And all the people we lost this year Barry White, Gregory Hines, The fat dude on that show What's Happening Re Run, John Ritter, Nell Carter, Bob Hope just so much is going on? Fuck your right Rhonda said; what a difference a day make.

Now you know that Michael Jackson is back in news Ten-year later accused of the same bullshit.

Christina talked on the phone as she walked around her room taking off her work clothes.

Girl how was work Rhonda asked?

Things at work are good My Children's program is the talk of the medical circuit I had a

Call from an Ms Jones about interviewing me on how to set up a program for her Hospital.

I'm impressed Rhonda said.

I also have fifteen new volunteers this year.

Christina walked into the bathroom to turn on the water for her bath she walked over to the cabinet in the bathroom to get her lavender bath beads to put in the water.

Girl I'm so ready to relax as she put the Lavender candle on the side of the tub

So how are things in St Louis?

I love it here; things are great.

How is the new man in your life?

Rhonda asked to break the tension.

If it had not been for the lord, Kenny the my parents I just don't know

He's wonderful Kenny has been every thing good girl I think he's the one.

Your kidding, you took the wall down from in front of your heart.

Yes girl and it feels good.

Christina said as she stepped in to her bath and lay back on the plastic bath pillow.

At first my intention was to just go out on a few dates, but I have really started to fall for him it's been five months and I'm on top of the world with this part of my life

You haven't let a man in your life for years Rhonda said.

Men were never off limits its just work was more important. Christina said.

Yhea right; Rhonda said

Your ass was through with the men specious; who do you think your talking to.

Kenny has been great he has opened me up in more ways than one girl.

I bet he has. Rhonda said

I have never had a man love me with so much passion it feels like we both need each other when were together.

You know what I mean?

Sometimes you can say to someone damm I needed that but when were together it's like he needs me just as much as I need him.

That's the best part about it. Christina said and smiled to herself just the thought of Kenny made her happy.

Damm like that? Rhonda said.

Yeah.

You know it like when we went to the gym that time you had a head cold and we went into the eucalyptus steam room and all of a sudden your head was clear.

He's just like that to me a breath of fresh air.

That's cool girl I need to keep the fire in my relationship with Tyrone burning.

Tyrone is still doing well; His business is doing real good and the girls are getting so big.

That's good Christina said.

How are my beautiful goddaughters?

There perfect, things are well.

Great give them a big hug for me.

Sure thing.

Hey! Do me a favor tell Tonya I send my love?

You take care and I'll keep you in formed with any up dates.

I just need to set here in this bath and soak.

Girl and I have to cook dinner and get ready for my tomorrow so I'll talk with you later Rhonda said.

Bye.

Bye, Christina said.

That night Christina slept throught the night with out one single nightmare.

She had been having them often after Tonya's ordeal.

Christina you have a call on line two Kim's voice came in loud over the intercom

Thank you Christina said as she pushed the intercom button on the phone.

Christina this is Montana Jones I work with Mercy Hospital Child program we talked on last week. I need to talk to you about your children's program. Will you still be able to meet with me Thursday?

Yes. Christina said with excitement. I would love to help your new program get off the ground

Well we at Mercy heard great things about your children program and how it has helped a lot of the inner cities sick Children.

It is our dream to become an extent ion of your program but at another Hospital.

Mr. Gardener I'm Matt the man standing there with his hand stretch out said to Milo.

Matt how can I help you. I'm with Citie Bank we are financing your construction project.

I have the paper work you need to sign.

Come this way with me and we can do this in my office.

As Milo enters his trailer's office his phone was ringing.

Hello.

Milo it's me dad the detective has some news for us and he wants to meet with the family this evening what time will you be off?

I can be out of here by three pops.

That's fine son, meet your mother at the house and I'll be there by four.

Okay pops I'll see you then.

Detective Dent met with the family that evening; we tracked the suspect to a location In the Wiltshire Dist.

A young lady was found in an empty Condo last week and it looks like our guy is up to his old tricks.

Is she all right?

Yes she is she was badly beaten just like Tonya and left for dead she was also raped and her personal things were missing.

Oh Lord Mrs. Gardener shouted!

Mom Milo said as he went to her chair and placed his arm around her.

Father in heaven please let them catch him.

Mom they will if they don't you can bet I will.

Boy you just stay out of it, Mr. Gardener said.

Detective Dent looked over at Milo.

We are closing in on him it's just a matter of days.

I needed to tell you all this in person before the media put the story out about the young lady we found.

The young lady is in critical condition we are hoping that she recovers, she was beaten so badly.

Her parents flew in from Washington State last night their daughter was her going to school USC.

With the budget crisis I really don't see how the students can afford to attend these schools. It wasn't like that when my children were in college. Mr. Gardener said.

That's true pop. Milo Said.

With all the California State University system-approving fee hikes it's going to be hard.

Well people I need to get back to the office and meet the press about this new case, I'll keep you good people informed with any up dates. Detective Dent said as he reached to shake Milo's hand and then Mr. Gardener hand.

Mom I'm going to the Hospital I'll see you all later.

Milo went to spend some time with Tonya before he turned in for the night.

Hello;

Hi baby.

Kenny how are you dear?

I'm missing you girl.

I miss you to, when will you be back?

Tomorrow sweet heart.

How was your day? Kenny asked?

It was busy I'm a little tired lonely, and sleepy.

I miss you and I need to be in your arms right now. Christina said teasingly.

Baby that's not fair you're messing with my head girl.

Do I need to catch a red eye to LA tonight or will you hold out until tomorrow?

Kenny asked playfully.

Are you coming back tomorrow? Christina asks with excitement in her voice.

Yes that's what I called to tell you before you started teasing me.

What time?

About noon, Kenny said.

I think two weeks is to long for us to be apart so from now on I'm only going to take a day or two when I need to be gone because I miss my girl to much.

And I miss you to sweetheart. Christina said as she sat on the edge of her bed looking across the room into the mirror.

She looked at herself and thought he does love me and she could see the joy that she felt inside.

How is Tonya?

She had a good day today. She's still not out of the woods yet.

Her Doctor think she's still in danger, she still has a little swelling around her brain.

I'm sorry to here that baby, I feel for here.

Baby how was your day? Christina asked trying to change the subject she did not want to feel bad and he was so far away.

Things are almost finished with this case and I'll be filling the last court papers and I'll be finished.

This guy parents want me to appeal the judgment but it's no use its over he has Ten years and that's that.

I'm coming home Kenny said.

Ms Gardener woke early this morning with a feeling that some thing was not quite right.

Lord bless this day father, thank you for another day and keeping me and my family safe through the night.

She said as she went into the rest room to brush her teeth and get dress for the day.

After dressing she headed down stairs for coffee.

Milo and her husband left early for work, but the coffee pot still had hot coffee in it for her.

Mrs. Gardener drank her coffee and look at the Loa Angeles Times news paper that Milo had left on the kitchen counter.

Headlines read 40 Killed in U.S Attack on Iraqi Border.

Mrs. Gardener arrived at the hospital about 9:00am Tonya looked stressed she thought.

Good morning a nurse said as she entered Tonya's room.

Good morning to you Karen, Mrs. Gardener said Tonya had been in the hospital so long she had gotten to know each nurse on every shift by their face and their first name.

Hey tell me something my daughter looks a little pail don't you think.

Let me check Karen said as she approached the bed.

Karen notice a pail completion just like Mrs. Gardener did.

Kern started checking all the monitors the I.V monitor was fine she walked over to the oxygen machine and it was fine also.

What is the matter Mrs. Gardener asks Karen just as the heart monitor started to beep! And flat line.

Karen ran to the door we need a team in here stat.

The nurses at the nurse's station heard the alarm and begin to run into Tonya's room.

Tonya was going into heart failure.

Help her! Help her Mrs. Gardener yelled.

Get the cart one nurse yelled!

Get her out of here another nurse yelled.

Help her! Help her Jesus help.

Get the crash cart HURRY.

Mrs. Gardener we need you to step out we have it under control the nurse said as she walked her out.

Call Doctor Freeman Now! Karen told the nurse at the nurse station. Dr Freeman we have a code blue! Dr Freeman we have a code blue on the Third Floor.

Clear! The nurse said as she worked on Tonya.

Doctor Freeman ran in and took over.

Pump! Clear! Flat line no heartbeat.

Pump! Clear! Flat line no heartbeat.

That's all you could here.

The machine still had a flat line on it.

Pump! Clear!

Beep, Beep, Beep.

She back Doctor Freeman said.

Good work people, Doctor Freeman said.

Was any family member here when this happen?

Yes Doctor Her mother is sitting out there.

Oh God, I think you need to call her brother and let him know what happen and have him come and sit with the mother I know she pretty shook up.

Milo felt his cell phone vibrate in his pant pocket; he reached in and pulled it out.

The caller ID read Daniel Freeman Hospital.

Milo stomach tighten just that fast.

Hello.

Mr. Gardener please.

This is he.

Mr. Gardener I'm Karen at Daniel Freeman Hospital-

What's the matter Milo Yelled into the cell phone?

Your sister went into heart failure—

What!

I called to tell you—

What! Milo Scream is she all right?

Mr. Gardener calm down I need to finish what I'm trying to tell you.

Is my sister all right?

Yes.

But your mother was here when it happen I need for someone to come and sit with her she is very shaken—

I'm on my way click.

Milo rushed through the automatic doors at the hospital ran through the lobby heading straight for the elevators.

Milo looked extremely nervous.

Mrs. Gardener was seated in the waiting area all shaken up; she was rocking back and forth.

A lady that was there waiting for a friend to come from her visit with a sick relative came over and placed her arm around Mrs. Gardener and said it will be all right honey.

It will be all right she said sympithicly God is a merciful God.

Milo blinked hard and swolled all his fear perspiration began to soak through his shirt as he walked towards the waiting area.

Milo saw his mother sitting there with the woman in a blue dress he did not recognize her as one of his relatives. He acknowledges his mother fear right away.

Hold on mom he said with sadness.

Mrs. Gardener sat motionless on the chair near the window in the waiting area, her tears bubbled and fell from her eyes as she screamed inward.

This was very hard for Milo to see time and time again the tears and pain that was coming from the strongest woman he'd every know.

Milo shook inside from the pain he felt for his mom, but he had to stay strong for her.

We are losing her she kept repeating in her head through the blur of her tears she looked up and spotted Milo, where is your father she said softly?

Milo felt a rush of tears form in his eyes; He's on his way he said as the tears fell from his eyes.

Milo know all to well that Tonya was a fighter and if she had any strength she was working hard to come back to them.

If God allowed it she would pull through this, but was his mother strong enough this was breaking her bad.

Milo had to remain mindful that he and Tonya came from this woman and she is a very strong woman.

This was breaking her down he thought to himself.

Weary with emotions Milo excused himself from his mother and the lady in the blue dress to go find the Dr.

With emotions nearly getting the best of him Milo went into his sister room anxious to make sure she was still hanging in there.

After seeing his sister Milo breathed a sigh of relief she looks ok he thought to himself a good feeling came over him it was as if he felt Jesus speak right in to his ear telling him that its all ready alright, she will survive he heard himself say as he bent down over the bed rail to kiss his sister face and whisper in her ear come back its all good I know you are going to be alright I can feel it.

When Milo was a child he use to get this same feeling about things.

There was a time that his father got hurt really bad at work and he was rushed to the Hospital.

He had slipped and fell hitting his head so hard that he was in a coma for a month.

It was touch and go the Dr. told his mother they did not know if his dad would make it.

During his comatose stage he had a stroke and things did not look good.

Milo went to visit him one day at the hospital and that was very hard for him to do but he did.

Mr. Gardener laid there very still Milo talked to him for hours at a time, and then some thing came over him a overwhelming good feeling like as he call it a visit from Jesus,

He told his mother that Jesus came in just as he was praying for dad and he said to him that it's all right your dad will live again a full and healthy life all is well he heard the voice say.

Mrs. Gardener knows that her children know the lord but this was way out she thought silently.

Milo was only twelve and his father was his life he was bigger than the greatest supper hero to his son.

Mrs. Gardener believed Milo when he told her that dad would be all right because she wanted that too more than life itself and she prayed for it just like her son did but she heard no voices.

The next day the Hospital calls the house bright and early with the good news that Mr. Gardener had came out of the coma and the symptoms of the stroke had all appeared as if nothing happened.

All was well and he was released a day later with his mind and memory in tact.

Tonya lied there fighting for her life. Milo kissed her face and left the room to find the Dr.

Mrs. Gardener shivered as she relived the seen from this morning at Tonya's bedside.

Mr. Gardener had arrived and was seated by her side as she told him what had happened.

Milo did not find the Dr so he decided to go tell his mother what he had just experienced

Milo entered the waiting room to find his father and mother sitting talking about Tonya Hey pops he said excitement.

Mom it happened again!!

What she said with fear in her voice thinking Tonya had another bad episode.

Milo looked over at them in his opinion his pops was the strongest man he had ever known but he had showed weakness at that moment and the moment he heard that Tonya was found beaten and now that we almost lost her pops just looked defeated.

This had weaken his father considerably Milo strong tower was weakening this crisis was affecting his parents bad.

Anguished he rubbed his hand over his face to clear his thoughts.

Mom I heard the voice again this time she believed him she know that her son was telling the truth she had believed that a manifestation of God grace was on the way.

Milo Face looked so sure and his voice spoke volume that the lord was working on the things that was pertaining to his sisters well being.

Mr. And Mrs. Gardener and Milo prayed and agreed that it was already all right.

Over the next few weeks the family came and went from the hospital with great expectations things were looking up.

Things had gotten a lot better as the weeks past Milo hooked up with one of the nurses

On the day shift, Mr. And Mrs. Gardener was feeling in great sprits now that Tonya had

Woke up from her coma Dr. Freeman had realized that he was falling for Tonya.

Christina had noticed that Dr Freeman was spending a lot of his personal time just sitting in her room.

Man Christina thought what a difference a day make's.

Christina entered the waiting room area of her office to her surprise Kenny was

Standing there with beautiful flowers in hand and a happy smile on his face

She screamed and ran into his arms.

Hay baby—damm girl I miss you, do you have time to go for lunch?

Yes sweetheart just let me put these in my office.

Thank you baby the flowers are beautiful.

Just like my girl Kenny said with joy in his voice.

Tonya was feeling pretty good these days and her injuries were healing up just fine she

Was almost feeling like her old self-things were looking up for her.

Ring, ring, ring.

Hello hay how is my favorite patient?

Tonya held the phone away from her face smiled and covered her mouth and made a little scream into her hand damm its Dr Freeman.

Hello she heard the voice on the line say.

Oh hello I'm fine Dr, How are you doing she asked trying not to sound excited.

What is he calling me on this phone for she thought to herself, where is he, and what do he want I hope its me in his bed thought she to herself.

Oh yeah I'm back a voice said in her head as she smiled to herself.

Tonya you sound real good today I thought I would call and check on you.

Do you call all your patients on their room phone and check on them like this?

Say no Tonya said to her self.

Tonya was really digging this man he's bright, handsome, has a good job, no ring on, and fine as hell all 6ft 5inches of him.

Well no I'm busted I was just concern about you today and scence I'm out of town at a conference I wanted to make sure that you were all right.

Yhea right brother your fine ass is liking me like I like you admit it she said to her self.

Oh that's nice of you Dr but you could have gotten that information from one of your nurses.

I got you now mister Tonya laugh to herself he must be shy I'll play along.

Well your right but I wanted to talk to you.

And so you are Tonya said with a sexy tone in her voice.

Dr Freeman could feel beads of sweat starting to form on his forehead something inside

Of him moved.

This was a woman that he truly wanted to know better; he was breaking all of the rules his rules never date a patient or a staff member.

Well miss lady you sure sound a lot better.

And I feel a lot better too when can I get out of here?

Dr Freeman thought to himself not until I get back for sure.

Tonya is a keeper he thought and he was going to be the man to keep that beautiful woman for always.

Tonya I feel you need to stay a little longer there are a few more test that I need to do on you.

I have a few test that I can do on your ass to Mr. man Tonya said to herself with a smile across her face.

Well I see Dr she said politely.

Tonya, Dr Freeman said than stopped.

Yes, she said with anticipation.

Mylz she heard a voice say.

Yeah Jack.

Man the conference is about to start up again lets go bro.

Hey Tonya I have to get back in there is it all right if I call and check on you tonight.

Yes you're the Dr she said playfully.

I'll call you back I promise.

Good buy Tonya said.

Good buy Dr Freeman said with sadness in his voice.

Tonya held the phone in her hand and look at it for a minute that was a strange call she

Thought did he want to tell me something or what.

Privately she thought to herself how can he like me after all of this?

Maybe my mind is playing tricks on me, or maybe I'm just dreaming.

Tonya shook her head.

Tonya vaguely remember any thing after the chocking and the blows to her face after that everything else is a blur.

She'd wonder about this for a long time, right now she just wanted to rest.

Christina sat there starry eyes at how handsome Kenny was to her, He just took her breath away with the little things he would do to make sure she was happy.

Kenny talked a little about the case that had just ended and how he was finish moving all of his things to the L A office.

I'm impressed with your work sweetheart Christina said with admiration.

Your absolutely amazing sweetie she said.

Kenny asked Christina how was Tonya doing and her family.

There fine things are really looking up in the Gardener family; Milo started dating a woman from the hospital one of the day shift nurses a pretty young lady, pop and mom

Gardener are in good sprit.

Tonya on the other hand is getting back to her flirty self, You know that Dr. Who's in charge of her care I think he has a thing for my girl Christina said, how

Ever I don't know if it's too soon for her to be getting involved with any one right now.

Why Kenny asked with concern in his voice.

If that happen to me I would never want to be around a man again.

Kenny shook his head.

You

Don't have to worry about that sweetheart I'll protect you always he said finally.

Christina thought to herself just the way he said that she knows it was the truth.

Sis are you woke?

I'm woke Milo Tonya said sounding as if she had just fallen asleep.

I just stop by to visit.

Yeah-right Tonya said in a playful way.

Girl you know that you're my favorite girl next to your mama.

Boy what's up Tonya said as she reached for the water that sits on the bedside table.

Your ass know your waiting for that little nurse what's her name Tonya said with raised eyebrows.

Girl please you think you know me; I was in the neighborhood.

Hey guess what happen you know Dr. Freeman my Dr right.

Yeah Milo said what's up with him?

Well today was weird he called me on this phone Tonya said as she pointed at the phone.

It was crazy he said that he's out of town and he wanted to check on me.

Why didn't he call the desk and ask one of the nurses at the nurse station Milo asked with concern.

I was totally shock I thought that it was you are mommy calling to check on me.

Well what did he say?

Just that he wanted to call and check on me and that he was out of town and maybe I can be released soon after a few more test.

A few more test; it seem like they gave you all the test in the world already Milo said as he put the magazine down and walked to the door of the room and looked out for the third time.

Brother Tonya said sweetly who are you looking for?

After Lunch Kenny and Christina went back to the hospital.

In the parking lot Kenny got of the car to let Christina out, well sweetie will I see you tonight he asked.

Yes I'll be leaving here about four and I'll pick up a few things and make you a home cook meal for your first day back.

Damm girl what did I do to deserve you.

Baby kiss me so I can get back to work Christina said in a sexy tone.

Kenny bent down and took Christina face in both hands and kissed her immediately

Christina felt moisture form in between her legs it's been awhile Kenny had been gone for three weeks and she was well over do.

Kenny kissed her soft and slow his tongue teasing hers every part of him wanted her right here right now.

Kenny reaction to what he was doing made Christina feel good she heard Kenny groan and moved in closer so she could feel what she was doing to his more sensitive part of his anatomy.

Kenny whispered in her ear baby I'll be there at six and I'll be spending the night unless you have some objections.

His hands held her close to him, Okay lets get back to work Christina said with affection.

Kenny tried to catch his breath your right I'll see you soon.

Christina made her way back to her office and thought to herself let me go check on my girl.

Just as she turned to leave out of her office the phone rang.

Hello hey girl what's up?

Tonya girl I was just thinking about walking up there as a matter of fact I was just on my way.

Okay well I'll see you in a minute Tonya said happily.

As Christina made her way through the hospital she ran in to a young lady with tears in her eyes.

Miss are you all right may I help you with something Christina asked.

Do you work here?

Yes I—.

I was just beat by a man.

What! When?

Wait come with me I'll get you some help.

Linda! Christina call to the woman at the desk, take this woman to the exam room over there please.

I also need you to get in touch with that Detective that was here working on the Gardener case please.

Christina drew in a deep breath she was feeling heated inside she needed to calm down

She immediately felt chills come over her.

I bet it's that same bastard that did this shit to Tonya.

That mutherfucker boy if they catch his ass he's grass I hope I'm there to see his sick ass.

I'll be his worse nightmare; I'll be the fucken check that over draws his fucken account.

Wait you just wait.

Christina needed to calm herself down breath girl breath she kept repeating to herself.

Christina walked back into the room.

Sweetie I'm Christina she said softly to the young lady; can you tell me what happen.

Or would you like to talk to one of the social workers.

Please I don't want to talk to anyone can I tell you, are you a Dr. the young lady asked still shaken.

No I'm one of the Administrator of this hospital its okay.

This girl had to be about mid Twenties 5ft 4inches brown almond face with beautiful slanted eyes, long curly hair and a nice firm aerobic body.

She was dressed in a nice Donna Karen suite with nice pumps on that match her suite looking real business like.

May I ask your name Christina said softly?

Angela Hill.

All right Miss Hill can you tell me what happen? Take your time.

Angela took in a deep breath before starting.

She sat shaking on the bed in her paper dress as they waited for the Dr. to come.

Angela started to talk to Christina she felt comfortable around her even though she had just met her.

Her fear quickly gave way to peace and calm.

Christina reached over and touched Angels hand take your time.

Christina gave her a friendly little squeeze it's all right now.

Start with telling what you do for a liven.

This was not the normal thing to ask but Christina felt this had some thing to do with Tonya beat down.

I'm a new Realtor with Home Mate.

Christina reacted when she told her that, her suspicions were confirmed.

Angela went on to tell her that she had a client to meet and show some property to about nine this morning.

She went to meet with this person but she was not going to show him the places; she had to cancel.

I tried to phone him but he must have all ready left for the meeting spot so she had to drive over there.

Upon arriving there she notice a nice looking black gentleman sitting in a car.

She walked over to the car and asked him his name and introduced her self.

After that she told him that she was unable to show the property.

I explained that I tried to phone him she said through her tears.

Sweetie take your time.

By this time Detective Dent had arrived and joined Christina in the exam room.

He sat quite taken notes from the corner of the room looking at Angela and trying hard not to show how angry he was that this guy is still out there.

Angela wrapped her arms around her self to study her shaken.

Do you need to take a break Christina asked?

No I'm fine.

Do you need a blanket Miss Hill Detective dent asked with compassion?

Yes please Angela said softly.

Angela continual with what went on after a few minutes.

As I was saying Angela said. I was just standing by his car and out of no where he punch me right on the left side of my head.

Quickly before I know it he hit me again and again I tried to scream she said firmly I tried I tried to scream she kept saying.

Detective Dent approach quickly and sat in the chair near the bed.

Are you okay Detective Dent asked politely.

I tried to fight back he was chocking me I scratched his face real good she said.

Detective Dent jumped up when she said that.

I need to get you checked your fingernails might still have his skin underneath them.

Detective Dent went over to the door open it and yelled for a nurse to come in quickly.

Tina a head nurse was at the desk she came in with the quickness.

How can I help you? She knows who Detective Dent is a lot of the nurses did.

I need to get her hands and nails scraped right now.

Okay I'll send a lab tech in right away

I scratched him with my right hand, I heard him say bitch; I'll kill you all of you bitches.

He kept hitting and hitting me lord I wanted to die.

Soon her reality returned she had been beaten bad her face started to hurt. Her head had knots all about the front and back and the pain was real the swelling came fast.

After I kneed him in the growing he let go I jumped up and ran I made it to my car and drove myself here.

I feel that if it wasn't for us being on the streets he may have killed me.

The look on his face; he wanted to kill me it was as if he know me or I reminded him of someone he must have known.

I apologize for all that has happen to you Detective Dent said to Angela.

I'll be one of the Detectives working on this case.

Taking Angela damp hand, You're frightened and you have every reason to be.

Talking to you helps Angela said calmly.

Dent put a protective arm around her shoulder; He was burning with rage in side.

How could some one be so cold, who could be so heartless and cruel to woman.

Angela please tell me any thing you can remember.

What sensations are you feeling think of any thing please any thing that can be useful a touch, smell, a sound you might have heard anything he asked gently.

Detective Dent sat in the waiting area try to get a grip on himself this is happening in his town on his beat; He sat nostrils flaring trying to suppress his anger I need to catch this fucken bastard enough is enough he slipped this time and this one got away.

Detective Dent called his office and asked for a 24hr watch over Angela room; make it a plain-clothes cop.

I know this one you will be looking for he told himself she did you some damage.

No one else has been able to tell us anything about this guy yet.

Detective Dent cast a whole net on the city of Los Angeles; He was expecting to catch a big fish.

Christina became a bit weary when she had awakened; she had tossed and turned all night thinking about Angela. She dreamed that she had caught the person that beat her friend.

Christina caught him and beat him down bad. She was drained from all of the fighting she had done.

Enveloped in a bath full of lavender bath beads and warm water she felt relaxed as she sat back.

In her mind she remembered the entire dream from last night, she had meet a man at an office on Vermont Avenue.

After getting to the office she noticed that it looked a little abandon except the office he gave me instruction to come to.

Christina noted that down on her note pad and stuck it under the passenger seat.

Christina entered the building and took in all of its features just in case this was the guy every one was looking for.

She walked up to the door and knocked.

Good morning she heard the voice say as a tall black man opened the door.

And good morning to you Christina said in her friendly tone; Are you Mr. French.

Shacking hands Mr. French and Christina talked for a while about the property that she would be showing and than they walked out of the building.

After talking with him Christina thought to her self I can take him if he try something.

On the way out the door Mr. French turned slightly to the right Christina noticed a long scratch on the side of his face and two little scratches on his neck.

Oh shit Christina said inside of her self he is the one; stay cool you can take him but wait be sure.

Are you ready he said in his deep voice as he pointed towards the door?

Yes.

Would you like me to drive he asked delicately.

Excuse me; Christina said looking up from the papers she was pretending to be looking over.

Well I'll drive my car and you follow, I have another person to meet right after you and it's by the last house she said politely.

All right I'm right out front.

Mr. French she thought six feet tall dark brown skin, cold dark narrow eyes, well dressed, but if he was going to try some thing I was ready, After a year of Billy Blake's Tae Bo I could put up a good fight and fear is not even in this picture she said to herself.

I'm parked right over their Mr. French said pointing to a car three cars from hers.

Okay I'm right here Christina said as she stepped off the curb and walked to the driver side door.

Christina got in the car and dialed Milo.

Ring, Ring, Ring.

Yeah talk to me Milo said.

Boogie it's me Christina. She and all of the family called Milo by his nickname

What's up sis?

I got him.

Got who?

I'm about to show this man a house over on the west side he has scratches on his face and neck like Angela described.

Sis have you lost your mind your not a Realtor.

Boogie I have Tonya lock box key and I have been showing homes all week waiting for this Motherfucker.

Milo jumped up from his chair are you sure?

Boogie I think so I m sure.

Call the gang and meet me at 4572 Van Ness Ave the back door is open it should take you ten min.

Milo called every body in a ten min radius to get over to the house.

Christina pulled up to Mr. French's car and apologized for the delay and then they were on their way.

After arriving at the address Christina notice Kenny and Milo cars parked down the street.

Christina pulled up in the drive way and notice that Mr. French pulled up behind her.

They both exited their cars and headed for the front door, Christina pulled out Tonya lock box key and placed it on the box and the key tray popped out.

Christina asked courisly how do you like the front of this home?

It has a nice big front yard and beautiful land landscaping.

Yes it does Mr. French said I'll have a lot of yard work to do he said with a little laugh.

How old is this home Ms Taylor he asked interested.

Its Ten years old it's about twenty five Hundred square feet, new carpet through and new tile lets go in.

Milo, Kenny, Steve, John and Joe had arrived and stashed them self through out the house in hopes this was the guy that had beaten his sister and the rest of the woman this would be his last day of freedom.

Christina entered the house.

Its beautiful Mr. French said I like the white tile in this entry.

Over her is the liven room its very spacious as you can see Christina said.

Yeah your right Mr. French said playfully I could see my self in this.

In here we have the Kitchen its around this wall.—Hey!

Ouch Christina felt a punch right up side the back of her head and the she felt him pull her hair.

That was the wrong move every since she was young she hated to have her hair pulled.

Christina got her focus and did a Billy Blake's Tae Bo back kick right into Mr. French stomach and sent him flying into the dinning area.

This made him angry he charged at her with full force.

He ran at her and she did a sidekick and then a set of punches that backed him up he was very surprised she was not scared she wanted to fight.

He came at her again just as she got ready to throw another punch Milo and all of the boys were on his ass.

Milo punched him in the face, John hit him in the stomach, Kenny was throwing punches to his back and Christina did he famous kicks blood flew everywhere.

Steve was yelling hey! Hey guys your going to kill him stop that's enough it not worth it call the police. Mr. Motherfucken man how do you like this you punk ass bitch, get the fuck up Milo said get your ass up your ass is dead.

Milo snatched him up by his suit jacket and slammed him on the wall.

Sis call detective Dent.

Get him here quick and let him know the deal.

Milo and Kenny stayed with Christina until the cops and Detective Dent came.

By this time Christina had to look like she was attacked she needed to rip her shirt or at least look a little battered because Mr. French was beat the fuck up how was she going to explain the unexplainable she did not do all this damage.

He only got one punch in and pulled her hair before, all hell broke loose on him.

So she tried to look a little more messed up but the more her head started hurting from the one punch the more she wanted to kick his ass.

Christina winced with horror after she realized what had just happen she could have been killed.

Ring, Ring, Ring the alarm went off good lord I'm glad it was a dream.

Dr Freeman returned Thursday and went into the Hospital early than usual, hello Dr.

Nurse Kim said as the Dr. passed that nurses station Kim also had a little crush on Dr. M Freeman. She started a month ago and she took a liken to Dr. Freeman immediately.

Dr. Freeman headed to Tonya room it was early he had hope to catch her sleeping.

He loved to set by her bedside and look at her beautiful face while she sleeps.

Tonya was a very beautiful woman to Mylz he thought if she only knew how he had fallen for her.

Mylz stepped into the room quietly trying not to wake her and to his surprise she was sitting in a chair on the other side of the room next to the window with her back to the door reading a newspaper.

Dr. M Freeman stop short of entering after he spotted her there with her back turned and just took in her beauty.

Who's there she said with out turning around?

It's me Dr. Freeman.

How are you? Tonya Said as she turned and placed her new's paper on the chair.

Tonya had been up for hours she couldn't sleep she knew that the Dr. was returning today and she wanted to look nice when he came.

Milo had brought her some of her clothes some dresses she could slip on nothing too much since she had been feeling better.

She turned to face the Dr. and his eyes open so big she thought some thing was wrong.

Tonya was looking good her makeup was applied nicely on and her hair was combed her beautician had came to the hospital to hook her up, her dress is a linen white with spaghetti strap knee high dress that fit every curve.

Tonya Dr. Freeman said shacking himself out of his trance, your up early how do you feel?

I'm great I just want to go home and get back in the swing of things she said happily.

Come sit down young lady Dr. Freeman said playfully.

Tonya came over to the bed and sat on the edge what are you going to do?

Well I want to check you out, I mean check your eyes and listen to hear what you got going on inside.

I'm fine you sure are he said under his breath you smell beautiful.

Thank you Tonya said calmly, what are you wearing you smell good to.

Oh I have on Aramis it's been around for years.

Tonya closed her eyes while Dr. Freeman took his tethascope and listen to her chest.

Tonya envision Dr. Freeman kissing her and holding her in his arms he's a great person she thought to herself caring, mature, handsome and really different I know he's not on the clock yet she told herself because he's not wearing his white lab jacket name tag or anything that would let you know he's a Dr.

May I ask you something Tonya said with a smile?

Any thing Mylz said.

Well I have too things.

Okay.

What time do you start work today?

Mylz wonder why had she asked that. Why do you ask?

You are usually in a lab jacket and looking like a Dr.

Number two what is your first name all I remember is seeing is M.

Well the truth is that I don't start work until Tomorrow.

And my name is Mylz Freeman.

Anything else?

I like that name she said sweetly.

What bring you here today?

I have a chance to catch up on some paper work he said, but was not being true full.

Tonya laid back on the bed so Dr. Mylz Freeman could exam her stomach; she laid there and took in a deep breath while he touch her stomach pressing his fingers down gently.

Mylz wanted to tell her how she affect him, she invaded his every thought his every minute, his stomach was in knots her aroma was driven him crazy he looked at her body laying on the bed and all of her curves he know this is a woman he wants but he was not good at approaching woman

His studies kept him busy his school and college days, dating was never important to him.

A few blind dates his friends hooked him up with which was it nothing serious.

Christina had a chance to get by Tonya's room and visit with her.

Tonya asked what had taken her so long; Christina told her how she ran into a woman in the hospital hallway. She tells her that she thinks that the guy that assaulted her had struck again. I'm sure it's him.

Christina went on to tell her that Detective Dent was on the case.

What the hell is this mutherfucker problem, who the fuck do he think he is. Tonya was hot she broke out the book of cuss.

I so want to get out of here and do some kind of sting operation and catch this fool he is bout to get on my fucken hit list.

He caught me off guard I would have fucked him up that punk ass bitch you know I don't play that man hitting woman shit especially if the woman is me, my father taught all of us in the neighborhood to fight and fight well.

Christina laugh out loud, she remember the fighting lessons in the garage of Tonya's house.

Those were the good old days.

Tonya sat up in the bed; boy you can tell that she was feeling like her old self and that made Christina feel good.

In spite of her long day seeing Tonya back to her old self made her heart skip a beat.

Tonya was so touch and go for a long time; to see her so alert and energized was cool.

Anyway Christina said this woman Angela got the best of this dude she said that she fought back and scratched his face real good.

The lab tech came down and took skin samples from her nails and we are going to run D&A samples on them.

Hopefully it will bring results before he strikes again.

Hold up you mean to tell me that he was not caught Tonya asked with disbelief.

Girl no she ran after he assaulted her and jumped into her car and drove herself to the hospital and we call the cops.

Wait she had a chance to run and she had a cell phone and did not call the cops.

What. You are not for real Tonya asked surprised.

If you would have seen how daze she was when she enter the hospital you would have known that she was not in her right mind.

Home girl is messed up, knots all up side her head, fear in her eyes getting out of this man area was her main concern.

I found her walking the hallway I asked her if I could help her, Christina said sadly.

She said that a man just beat her up.

Girl, than I found out that that she is a new Realtor and she meet this man to let him know that she could not show him the homes today and that set him off.

Why didn't she call him and tell him that Tonya asked softly.

She tried but could not reach him, so she decided to meet him and tell him in person.

I would have just stood him up Tonya said with out care as she shrugged her shoulders.

But you've been in this business for years you know that new Realtors chase the buyers.

Christina reminded her.

Yeah I guess your right.

So how is she doing right now Tonya asked with concern?

The detective is sill with her Christina said sadly.

How are you doing Tonya?

Oh! Guess what! She said with excitement as she bounced around on the bed.

You know that fine ass Dr.

Who Christina said with her eyes poked out.

Girl you have worked here for years you should have told me that it was a hot ass Dr. working here.

Who the hell are you talking about?

My Dr. Tonya said as she stood up and walked to the door and picked out.

Who are you looking for Christina asked with a smile on her face she remembered how they use to do that at Tonya's house when they talked about boys and she thought her mom was listening?

Christina laughs to herself.

Tonya closed the door and came back and sat on the bed.

Girl slow down Christina said, who is this Dr. That's got you all shook up.

Dr. Freeman she said with a big smile.

Mylz; Christina asked.

Who is Mylz Tonya asked; She had forgot that he told her his name earlier.

His name is Mylz your Dr. Name is Mylz Freeman.

Oh shit that's what the M is for, oh yeah I thought he said Mark or something like that.

He is cute in his on little way she said.

Cute Tonya yelled he is fine have you seen him with out his Dr. jacket on.

No.

Girl his body is banging.

Are you dreaming? How did you see him with out his Dr. jacket on?

He was here earlier and he was not on duty he came here to check on some paper work he said Tonya said with a smirk and her left eyebrow raised and head tilted.

Paper work my butt I think he has a crush on me.

You are crazy Christina said smiling.

The last I heard Mylz went to a conference with a couple of other Doctors from here.

I know he even called me from there to check on me.

Shut up Tonya your tripping.

Bitch I'm fine, my head is right and I know when a man is digging my ass and especially a rich man.

They both laugh simultaneously.

Okay Christina said, what's up?

I think he's a little shy.

But I heard that he was coming back from his trip today.

How did you here that Christina intruded?

I was listening to the nurses at the station as I passed by.

Any way I was not even tripping on him I seen him and didn't see him.

After he called and said he was checking on me I thought this is cool, and he was a little flirty.

I asked him why he didn't just ask the nurses how I was doing instead he called me on this room phone girl she said pointing at the phone by her bed.

You are kidding Christina said jumping in her seat now.

Well I guess your right she said.

Is that why you are in street clothes today?

Hell yeah I set the seen.

What happen? Christina asked with excitement because she knows her girl was no joke.

Tonya began tell her story about how she was sitting by the window after she picked out of the door and saw Dr. Freeman coming down the hall way towards her room.

She told her how she hit her toe on the bottom of the bedpost running so fast trying to get in the chair.

Girl I hit my toe so hard I could not sit in the chair fast enough so I stood by the window than sat in this chair because my toe was throbbing.

I was there making ouch faces at this newspaper I pretend to be looking at.

Christina's image of this was making her laugh so hard her stomach was hurting.

Tonya went on; obviously he was coming here, I had already told Milo to bring me some clothes from home because I was tired of wearing these hospital gowns.

I got up early and did my thing in hopes he would show up.

Just as I started to go on a walk around the hospital in search of a victim I spotted him.

Christina was grabbing her stomach laughing.

Girl he walked in and I could see his reflection in the window glass.

He stood there checking me out for a minute Tonya said shaking her head from side to side getting into her ghetto mold.

Quit it fool your killing me Christina said through her laughter.

Tonya was a real drama queen she had a way of pulling you right into the picture.

I go who's there, like I'm a little blind girl with out turning around, knowing I'm looking at his fine ass all the time Tonya said with a sneaky look on her face as she raised her one eyebrow.

It's me I heard his deep voice say.

Girl I got so wet in my good spot she said shaking her legs I thought someone throw water on me.

Tonya shut up Christina said laughing.

My stuff immediately got wet, girl I'm back Tonya said tilting her head to the side.

Anyway I turned around and the man eyes almost popped out of his head.

Why Christina asked exhausted.

Shit my ass was looking good, my make up was on flawless Janice came yesterday and hook up the hair, no more bruises, my clothes are on hit if I say so myself.

Yeah girl you do look rich and famous Christina commented, you look like miss thang again.

I also have the smell good on because I know he had to play if off and do his Dr. thang and check me.

You know the stuff they do.

I put on my best push up bra from Victoria Secret you know that high price one Tyra Banks advertises.

Shut up girl Christina was laughing again.

And he went to listen to my heart and saw both of the twins, he looked up so fast I thought he seen a ghost

Baby is a little shy Tonya said.

Then I laid back on the bed and he check my stomach just the way he touched me and stared at my body told me what he was thinking.

He wants me I'm sure.

Just as Tonya finished the story Mylz came knocking.

Knock, knock.

Simultaneously Tonya and Christina look at each other with raised eyebrows.

Come in Tonya said happily.

Dr. Freeman she said.

On the drive from the hospital the image of Kenny came to Christina she needed to talk to him and tell him about this crazy day.

After thinking she changed her mind.

I just want to be feed and made love to all night she said to her self after I soak in a hot tub.

Thoughts of Kenny filled he mind how he smell, his touch, how he lay his body on top of hers, how gentle he is when he make love to her.

Suddenly she felt a tingle her body was reacting to the thoughts of her handsome man.

Christina promptly pushed the image out of her mind she needed to get to the house and get ready for his arrival.

The chaos of the week was exhausting for her.

Kenny was on his way over and that's all she wanted to think about.

After taking a long bath Christina dried off and put on her lotion and nightgown.

Christina cell phone rang the caller ID read Kenny, Hi sweetie what's up? Kenny said.

Nothing She said as a big smile came across her face.

Christina looked in the mirror and saw how the sound of her man voice brought such a big smile to her face.

Baby are you ready for me? Kenny asked in a very seductive voice.

Baby are you ready for me I'm here fresh out of the tub lotion down naked and smelling good laid across the bed and I'm going to start playing with myself if you don't get here soon.

No baby I'm in the drive way don't touch a thing I'm here Kenny said with a rush sound in his voice.

Christina laughs to herself.

The front doors open, Just as Christina put on her silk robe and tied the belt.

She left the room to greet Kenny at the door but as soon as she entered the hall he was in her face.

Now what was that you were saying Kenny said with a huge smile on his face.

Christina reached up and put her arms around Kenny's neck and they kissed baby I missed you Christina said.

I had a tough day all I want is for you to put me to sleep or we put each other to sleep.

I'm cool with that Kenny replied as he picked Christina up off her feet and placed her gently on the bed.

He looked into her eyes and stared at her for a moment, what's the matter she asked?

You are so beautiful and so damm sexy and all of this Kenny said as he looked over whole body you give to me.

I just want to treat every inch of you with tinder love and care.

Damm that sound good Christina said to herself hurry up.

That nice sweetie she said, I Love you.

I love you too Kenny said as he began to unrobed Christina and kiss her neck, her chin, her lips, her chest and down to her breast he stayed there for a while licking up and down and around and around taking his time suckling each nipple.

The heat of his toung and breath was driving Christina wild.

Christina moan and groaned this made Kenny work harder he new that she was enjoying his work.

Christina rubbed his head and face as she called out his name.

Kenny continued down her body he licked softly and traced his tongue all over her stomach.

Christina moaned louder as he neared her wet spot she liked when he sucked her there.

Kenny took one hand and started rubbing her breast and the other hand he help himself entered her body.

Christina let out a loud groan and this made Kenny want to go in deeper the juice from her body was warm he push himself in and out her body talking to him each time he moved in and out.

Christina began to kiss his lips letting him know how much she had missed him today and that tonight was a night to remember.

She kiss his neck and worked her way down to his chest kissing, licking and suck each nipple and she licked her way down

Baby Kenny kept saying as sweat beaded from his forehead as his body moved up and back, like that baby that feels good.

This went on and on until we both exploded, we shook screamed and moaned this was good.

It was early morning when we fell asleep in each other arms.

Christina thought to herself as she was falling asleep if his Law practice is like his love making he is going to make his clients very happy the brother got skills.

Tonya called Christina office.

Hey you what's up Tonya asked cheerfully.

Girl not much just back to the grind I have a few things I need to check for the charity benefit next month.

Oh yeah Tonya said is their anything you need me to do?

Yes I need you to be feeling well and have your ass there.

Oh no problem I'm there, I'll be leaving here tomorrow if my handsome Dr let me leave.

Tonya said.

So what's up with that Christina asked.

He's been here every day two and three times a day poking on this or that I need him to Polk on my—.

Girl shut up Christina said as they both laugh simultaneous.

Yeah bitch your ready to go Christina said between her laughing.

Has Milo came through yet?

No, Tonya said why?

I need to see him if he comes have him come up and see me.

Is this about the little nurse he's seeing?

No Kenny wants to talk some business with him.

Oh Ok I'll let him know.

How's Kenny anyway.

Good girl real good.

Christina thought about all the time that she and Kenny had spent together and chills ran down her back.

He has never came half way he always make things look so easy.

Life with him would be so nice, he walk's in the room always bring something, he make love to your mind, body and soul like tomorrow might never come I can still feel him in side of me. She thought what a man as tingles ran through her private area.

Hello, Hello are you still their Tonya asked.

Oh yeah I'm here all right and feeling good.

You fucked last night and that man worked your ass didn't he Tonya said with excitement.

Girl! What are you talking about Christina said with a grin on her face.

Every time you get worked over miss thang you always do this drifting off thang

You remember the first time you did it with that boy what's his name and you came to school with that look on your face.

Back when we were in College I bet you have that look on your face now.

And you remember the first time you let Kenny hit that and your ass was just brain dead.

Tonya knew Christina very well.

Christina just laugh it was nice to have her best friend back and she was right Kenny had worked her over but if I feel like this what is he feeling like she thought to herself.

Ok girl shut up yeah it was one of those who can out do whom last night.

I work his ass and he worked me up and down.

Stop it Tonya said laughing I don't want to here it it's been to long I think my girl might be closed and cob webs are starting to form up around it.

I need out of this place Tonya said jokingly.

What about Dr Freeman Christina asked.

What about him?

I thought you had an eye for him.

I do I just need to get out of here so I can invite him home.

What do you want me to do here invite him to eat off my hospital tray?

They both laughed.

Girl shut up you are most defiantly feeling all right.

So when do you go home?

I think tomorrow he can't keep coming in here looking at my body for ever all the fake check up are almost old he has to come with a new game sooner or later or release me.

Knock, Knock May I come in the voice said.

Christina it's him he's here Tonya said excited I got to go.

Click, Damm Christina said you could a least let me say good by.

Christina laugh, Thank you Lord she is her old crazy self again.

Christina stood at the big window in her office that looks out over the city and thought about all of the events over the past few months and said time can be your friend.

All is well, what a differents a day makes.

Milo dropped in to see his sister and she told him that Christina needed to see him so before he leaves to go up to her office.

At Christina office he found her sitting behind her big desk working hard a phone in one hand and typing on her computer with the other.

Hey you come on in she said when she looked up and saw Milo standing in her door way.

What's up sis?

Well Mylz Tonya's Dr told me that he will be releasing her tomorrow and mom and I think we need to give a welcome home party.

Cool I'm down with that.

I'm thinking this weekend Christina said joyfully.

I'm free I'll make some calls and pull some of the old crew together and let them know Milo said.

After the party I plan a quite evening at her house with Mylz.

What? Milo said confused.

Oh you don't know about the crush that they both have on each other.

Oh hell no I in the dark.

Boy please they are liking on each other bad I think that a little help is in order.

There you go fixing people up again Milo said smiling.

Again what is that suppose to mean Christina asked with raised eyebrows.

Sis you know that girl friend you and Tonya had fixed me up with when I was in high school.

High School?

Yeah the ugly ass fat girl with the shorthair and thick glasses, the girl you and my sis felt sorry for at prom time.

Christina broke out laughing so hard she did remember the girl was tore up but she was nice.

Ha Ha Hell Milo said.

Christina kept laughing I'm sorry she said through her laugh.

Girl you're not right look at you your crying that's real funny.

Milo I had forgot all about that she said as she wiped the teas off her face.

Mylz is cool he really like's Tonya and I think she like's him as well.

Whatever Milo said, as he made a face at Christina.

Anyway do you know Christina asked that the girl you took out that night went on to become a top model in New York.

What?

Yeah she dropped all of the extra weight and got her eyes fixed and her teeth straighten and moved forward with her life.

Your kidding Milo said.

No I'm for real here is a photo on the cover of this magazine we spoke about four years ago all is well with her.

Milo looked at the picture it had no signs of a fat shorthaired four eyed girl from high school.

This woman here was thin tall body by fisher and a drop dead beauty man are you sure he asked.

I'm sure she said what a different a day makes.

Man I could get with this Milo said still looking at the beautiful woman on the cover of the magazine.

They say milk does a body good and she has too big milk bottles that will do me real good.

Boy shut up Christina said as she snatch the magazine from his hand.

Okay today is Monday and I have to call some of the girls from out of town and get them here it's not going to be a big, big party just about Thirty of our close friends.

So what do you need me to do Milo asked?

I need a list of all the family and close friends you think she would want to see.

No problem I'll have it for you tomorrow.

Milo Christina said it's a surprise I know that you can't hold water but don't let this slip out ok.

Girl that's the old Milo I'm a man now haven't you notice he said as he did a full turn in the middle of the room.

If you weren't like my sis you know you would be after me too he said smiling.

I see every one is back to there old self's Christina said to herself, Get out Milo I'll talk with you later this week.

I'm out I just need to pick up my cutie and I'm on my way later sis.

Dr Freeman came in the room Hey he said how is my favorite patient doing today?

(I'll be more than your favorite patient if you need me to be Tonya said inside herself.)

Fine, just fine Dr.

I have good news and bad news which do you want to here first.

(I hope the good news is that you are ready to take me I mean all of me and just do bad things to my mind and body Tonya said to herself.)

Well you chose which one I should here first Tonya said gracefully.

(Tell me you want to take me home and make love to me she said to herself as she look at Dr Freeman.)

Tonya did you here me he asked.

Sorry no what did you say Tonya asked shaken her head.

Are you all right Dr Freeman asked as he moved closer to the bed where she was sitting.

(Get your fine ass away from me I'm horny and hungry and you smell like something I can eat she said to herself).

I'm Fine Dr what did you say?

I said that your entire test came back and things look well.

That's the good news.

And the bad news is that I'm going to release you tomorrow.

That's not bad news that's perfect news to me I haven't seen my house for Eight months or my job I think that's wonderful new she said excitedly.

Through her excitement she notices a sad look on Dr Freeman's face.

(Oh this was bad new for you she thought to herself all you have to do is ask me out you block head).

Why was that bad new she asked Dr Freeman?

His face told her what his mouth could not, he was falling for her and he was falling hard.

He looked as if someone took his favorite toy from him.

He wanted her to stay but he had used up all the excuses and had run every test he could and there was nothing wrong that he could prolong her stay.

How could he let her walk out with out letting her know how he feels.

Dr. Freeman did you here me?

What?

I asked you why did you think that my leaving was bad new.

Tell me the truth and shame the devil you know you want me she said to her self.

Oh I said that because I'll miss not seeing you he said trying hard to smile.

(Oh you can see me all right all of me and feel me to whatever part you want she said to herself.)

I'm sure you have plenty of other patients that need you a lot more than I Tonya said in a playful voice.

(Not really I need you like a fat man need's cake, like cereal need's milk like ice cream need cake he said to himself.)

I'm sure your right, Ill miss you though I hope you keep in touch he said looking at Tonya.

I guess it's up to me Tonya told herself this brother must have some kind of rule about dating patients.

So tell me Dr. How do you want me to keep in touch Tonya asked seductively.

(You go girl she said to herself.)

Tonya was through with the cat and mouse games she knew he was digging her and she him.

Now that she is leaving the hospital there was no time for the games she had miss out on a lot in Eight months and now it was time to live I'm back and it feel's good thank you Jesus.

So how can a girl like me keep in touch with a busy man such as your self?

Dr Freeman forehead began to bead up with sweet he knew she had another side to her but he had only seen the quite shy woman in the hospital bed.

The voice of this aggressive person that wanted to know how to keep in touch with him was turning him on.

I'll give you my personal phone number, I really want to know how thing are going with you.

That's if it's all right with you.

(He's still playing with me Tonya thought to herself) I don't have time to waste I have been on hold to long this whole eight months was so real to me time waits for no one.

(Okay here it goes she said to herself.)

Tell me Dr. are you married?

Beep, Beep, Beep Dr. Freeman reached for his pager it's a page from the ER room

He rushed over to the bedside phone and picked it up and punched three of the numbers.

Yes Its Mylz, What do you have down there?

Okay I'll be right there Click he hang up the phone.

Mylz turn's and apologize to Tonya I have to get to the emergency room he start for the door.

Hey he said as he look over his shoulder the answer is no and I'll finish this conversation later if you don't mind he winks and out of the door he goes.

Tonya reaches for the phone to dial Christina just as she walks in the room.

Hey you I saw your man run out of here what did you say to him?

I told him I would give him some if he go right now and get me a room at the Marriott Hotel with a big Jacuzzi in the floor and some Champaign and bubble bath and he took off.

Christina started laughing you didn't did you?

No girl his beeper went off and he was needed in emergency.

So how are you? Christina asked.

All is well I got good news-

What Christina broke in and asked with excitement in her voice.

Girl I get to go home tomorrow I get to see my house, my car, my shower I'm so happy it's been a long time coming.

Thats great Christina said as she hugged Tonya.

Hey, I'll call a House cleaning crew to go over to your place and freshen thing up a bit.

You know your crazy brother has been camping out there.

Okay that cool that's less I'll have to do when I get home thanks.

Let's call now Christina said.

Christina picked up the phone and dial a service called we keep it clean there a very good cleaning service she uses some times.

Hello.

Regina how are you? This is Christina.

Hi Christina what can I do for you it's been a while?

Yes it has I have been in and out of town lately but all is well.

Good Regina said cheerfully.

What do you need?

I need a crew today if possible.

Sure I have some girls what time do you need them at your place Regina said with her heavy Jamaican accent.

No Regina I need a crew for my girlfriend I mean my sister's place.

Oh I see, give me the address and time you need them and I'll set it up.

Regina soon as possible she's leaving the hospital in the morning and I would like thing to be ready bright in early for her homecoming.

My brother should be home by three and he will let your girls in.

Ok we will be there.

Girl is she's all right.

Yes thank you she is doing much better.

Okay girl I'll send the girls over there what is the address?

Christina told her the address and arranged everything for Tonya.

Thank you Regina Christina said happily you're the best just send the bill to my office.

Tonya left the hospital the next day, ready but not ready at the same time.

How was she going to see Dr. Freeman again?

They had not exchange numbers and there were no more schedule visits.

(Oh well I guess it's for the best she thought) just as she said that to her self—

Dr Freeman walks into the room.

Excuse me he said in the sexiest voice she had ever heard you don't think your leaving here with out saying good by.

Tonya's back was turned he stood there looking her up and down wanting to walk over and place his arm around her small waist and pull her close to him.

Tonya smiled as she stared out of the window, damm she though that voice sure gives me special feeling's all through my body.

(Girl get a grip she told herself) while sharp tingles ran all through her body.

I was hoping you stopped by she said playfully.

Oh yeah he said surprisingly with a smile from ear to ear.

Tonya turned to see his face.

Yes I wanted to thank you for all the great care you really got me back in order.(In more ways than you think she said inside.)

As heat ran up and down her body from her toe to the top of her head as she looked into his beautiful eyes.

Tonya felt herself staring,(shake it off girl she told herself) and shook her head.

What's the matter Mylz asked after noticing her shaking her head do your head hurt?

(Yeah Tonya thought to herself and for all the wrong reasons).

No she said all is well, I fell just great she said smiling to herself.

Why do you ask?

(Damm he must have notice me shaking my head a girl got's to be more careful she said

Softly to herself.)

Oh I thought you were shaking your head because you were in pain.

No No I was just thinking.

(I hope it was something good about me Mylz thought to himself.)

Well Mylz said I owe all of the great care and hard work to the nurses and staff it was team work and your dedication to getting better that got you through this and let's not forget the Lord our god the all mighty because with out him you would not have survived.

But I'm very gald that you thought it was me.

(I would love to take care of you Mylz said to himself.)

(In all the right way, for all the right reasons.)

The way he looked at Tonya she knew he had to have said something to himself.

Why don't you just say you want me man Tonya thought I dare you.

Tonya was looking at Mylz when the thought crossed her mind her smile got wider.

So Miss Gardener where do you go from here?

I really know so little about you, (except what that beautiful face and body look's like he said to himself.)

Well sir what would like to know about little old me Tonya said playfully.

I'm single, live alone, as you can tell by now I have no children.

So I'm going home to try regaining some of my life back one moment at a time she said softly.

It was sad to hear that out loud she thought to her self.

May I ask you a personal question?

(Ask me out Tonya said to her self.)

Sure but I think you know all about me by now she said playfully.

I don't know if you have a man in your life.

Shock at his boldness Mylz stood there(okay I asked he told himself)as beads of sweat formed on his nose.

Tonya stood there looking at him(hell no I don't have a man she said to her self.)

Well no I don't I'm still single and looking she said smiling showing her beautiful white teeth.

Why do you ask?(Like I don't know she told herself).

Mylz took a deep breath and said so do this mean that I can ask you out.

At that very moment Tonya heart jumped so hard she knew that Mylz had seen it.

Tonya screamed so loud inside herself that she had to look behind her to see if the nurses outside her rooms were coming in.

Shocked at his own boldness he stood there waiting for what seem like hours waiting for an answer.

Tonya looked back around amazed the he had asked her out she didn't realize that her eyes looked as though she was in shock.

What was that look for Mylz asked? Was I out of line?

Oh no! She said quickly.

Walking closer to the Dr. I'm free she answered smiling showing all of her beautiful white teeth. When she stopped in front of the bed where Dr Freeman was standing every thing in her shook and her stomach was turning flips after flips(damm this man looks good to me she said to herself.)

How about Thursday today's Monday I'll give you a few days to do what you need to do relax a little and—

I would love to see you tomorrow if that's ok, If your schedule is not to full Tonya said with a serious look on her face. She didn't want to go another day and not see Mylz.

Don't you think I'm well rested?

Oh Oh yeah I mean oh no, no my schedule is really not full at all.

Tomorrow is fine he said smiling.

Tomorrow is good for me also but after I go and spend time with my parents.

And you will be free when he asks softly.

(I'll take the day off to be alone with you Mylz said to himself.)

Let's say I pick you up about six but I'll call you tonight to discuss our plans how about that.

That sounds perfect Tonya's said as she wrote down her phone number and address on the tablet that was near her bed.

Mylz reaches into his pocket and grabbed his cardholder and took it out and handed Tonya a card the card had his work, cell, and home phone on it.

All right six it is Tonya said in a flirty tone as she walked over to the window pretending to look out.

She knew that Mylz would be watching her, she wanted him to get one more good look at what he was about to get into.

As Tonya pass in front of Mylz the scent of her perfume caught his nose,(Damm he said

To himself) it's nothing like the scent of a woman.

Knock knock Milo came in what's up sis?

Hey Doc. What's up how's my sis?

He asked as they shook hands.

She's fine(in more way's than one he said to him self) he said as he looked at her smiling.

Ms Gardener I'll check in on you later Mylz said as he headed for the door.

Fine Milo said with his eye brow rose what was that about? Did I walk in on something? Oh yeah

Boy that's going to be my baby's daddy and my husband I think it's time for the old girl to settle down Tonya said shaking her head up and down.

Yeah! Milo said real loud thank you Jesus she's back.

Tonya if you date him more than two week's I'll be surprise.

Milo said shaken his head from side to side as he walked up and kiss her cheek.

Milo know Tonya's track record with men she only kept them for three weeks at the longest.

Being tied down was something she hated.

Milo recalled back in Fifth grade this dude name Travis use to always give Tonya things to get her attention like sunflower seeds, candy, his coffee cake at breakfast when we got to school early enough to eat breakfast.

We would always try to make it on Tuesday because that was the day the café served coffee cake and dude would be waiting.

At recess he would wait until she was alone away from her friend he would pass money to her while she sat on the bench.

At the end of that school year Tonya had at least Fifty dollars old dude was serious.

Tonya Kept all the money in an envelope under her desk stuck in the rail that held up the desk.

Tonya would say I hate Travis with his ugly self he keeps asking me to be his girlfriend, I like that new kid name Willie he just moved here from New Jersey.

Willie never notice Tonya at all he had his eye on the light skinned girl named Arletha

I thought that was pretty cool because it was the last day of school and we were walking and she said look at this.

I turned to see what she was talking about there it was a white envelope full of money coins and dollar bills from Travis. Tonya saved just in case he would ask for it back one day

Summer came and school was out Travis always would pass by our house and catch Tonya and Christina playing in the yard and stop to say hello, that really mad Tonya upset.

Christina would tease her saying here comes your boyfriend.

Christina and mom got thing ready for Tonya's homecoming party they made all the calls and ordered all the party trays, the DJ and bought all the drinks this was going to be a perfect party especially when mylz shows up.

Tonya got home and an hour passed she felt quite well especially after speaking to Mylz they talked briefly and hung up.

I just keep seeing his beautiful eyes and I want him bad. I want to feel him, smell him, be the wallet in his back pocket, and just be around him.

But why she thought to herself, is he my soul mate, I know he's feeling likes me, do I have brain damage. Man did homeboy fuck my head up when he beat me up? What?

I'm falling hard for Mylz I need to know why Tonya said looking into the mirror at her self.

After tomorrow I'll see what's up. I wonder if I'll even be comfortable alone with him outside for the hospital she said as she closed her eye's and tried to relax just as Mylz's vision, popped into her head.

Jesus I need you on this one Tonya said out loud. If it's your will, Tonya laid. Back on her pillow and closed her eyes.

Christina was home resting as she lay, on the bed she thought about all of the things that had happened these past months she reached for the drawer on the nightstand next to her bed to get her journal.

Dear journal she wrote today was very comfortable all is well with myself.

Kenny and I talked four times today and I feel that he's is truly haven sent I'm falling harder and harder for him his voice sends chills through my body still I dream of him I feel him in my private spot my nipples perk up when I hear him talk to me. Life is all to the good on the home front.

My girl Tonya got to go home today she was very excited I love that things are better for her she has come a long way I hope she and Mylz hook up. He will be good for her he might just be the challenge she needs.

I hope she finds love like I have. Well we have a party set for this weekend.

I came home and all went well. Christina, Milo, Mom and Dad came by for a while Tonya said to the person on phone.

Now I'm going to just take a bath and read for a while. I need to settle down from this day she said joyfully. So I'll talk you later and thank you for calling. Goodbye.

As she walked away she realized that she had come a long way. Tonya looked around her home. She was home and out of the hospital and it felt good.

Tonya stood in the living room and stared at all the beautiful things in her home that she worked so hard for. Her home was so peaceful Milo had bought her a beautiful bouquet of fresh flowers that sat on the table in the front of the couch the large white wall unit full of crystal was on the wall across the room from the couch and two large over stuff chairs sat on the other side by themselves.

Her floors are Cherry Wood throughout her house the kitchen floor is shiny brown marble with wedges of white marble radiating from the matching counter tops. She looked towards the dining area at the magnificent large chandelier that hung from the ceiling she remembered what seemed like forever for it to arrive.

For the first time in her life she felt lonely.

Totally independent was her model freedom to make her on decisions, pursue her own dreams and goals with sudden clarity came upon her she did not want to be alone all the months in the hospital with 24 hour visitors she now was home alone.

Dr. Freeman walked purposefully down the corridor towards the pharmacy to check on Tonya's medicine he ordered after she left the hospital he wanted to pick it up and drop it off at her home. He was missing her already.

Dr. Freeman picked up the medicine and headed for the stairwell that led to the lower level and parking garages he took the stairs everyday to keep himself in shape. With his busy schedule going to the gym was impossible so the stairs was a way of working out while he was at work for so many hours.

As Mylz got to the car he then removed his white coat and his ID. That read M. Freeman M.D. He then took off his stethoscope from around his neck and placed it in his briefcase that he carried.

As he drove out of the Dr. Private parking garage the parking attendant Joel yelled hay doc turn your lights on.

Mylz waved at him and turned the lights to the car on and drove towards Tonya's house.

Tonya was all he could think about he had fallen in love with her and it scared him. Unexpectedly she was the lady that grabbed his heart and he wanted so bad to see her again

Mylz reached into his pocket and pulled out the phone number she gave him before she left for home.

He opened his cell phone and dialed the phone number as the phone rang beads of sweat formed on his forehead and nose.

Damn, calm down boy he said to himself she's only a woman. The phone rang just as she steeped into her bath water. Tonya's caller ID read Mylz Freeman before she left the hospital she had programmed Mylz number into her phone this was truly a number she did not want to replace. After she sat in the hot tub of bubbles and water she answered, Hello she said trying not to sound excited because she was just thinking of him. Just seeing his name on the caller ID gave her goose bumps. This man is the one she thought all I need to do is break him off some of this good loving she said to herself.

May I please speak to Tonya Gardener he said. Oh No he's not trying to sound, all professional and shit she said to herself okay she thought.

Who may I say is calling she asked in a professional manner?

This is Dr. Freeman.

Tonya took the phone from her ear and looked at it with raised eyebrows what is this about she thought

Let me mess with his head. She said to herself

Splash Splash went the water loudly Dr. Freeman she said in a sexy manner this is Tonya

What can I do for you?

Oh did I catch you at a bad time Mylz heard the splash of the water and how seductive her voice sound he could only imagine how good her body looked naked and wet.

I just sat in the tub to wind down from this day. But it's okay

Did I forget something?

Mylz pulled his car over to the curb the sound of her voice and his own imagination was playing tricks on him.

He felt his body getting warm and his private part beating as if it had a heart.

No he said

I ordered some medicine and I really need you to start it today.

Well, Dr. Tonya said I'm sorry what is it for

Splash, Splash

It's for your, your

Dr. Are you okay Tonya asked. She know that she had him going

Yes

It's um antibiotics that's what it is Mylz said softly

Okay

Where do I need to pick them up, from

Mylz said I'm leaving the hospital now if it's all right I'll bring them by

Sure Tonya said excited.

Tonya kissed her phone after she pushed the hang up button. And said to herself that was not as hard as I thought it would be.

Cool he said to himself as he stared at his phone that wasn't as hard as I thought it would be, he turned up the music and pulled back into traffic headed towards Tonya's place.

Christina walked around her home wondering how blessed she was not to lose her best friend she had prayed for Tonya recovery she believed that miracles do happen.

Tonya was well and all is well and she is infatuated with Dr. Freeman I hope she and the Dr. will be good together.

Tonya never like being in relationships she only like the man for a few months because she said after a while with a man the sex plays out but if you date for almost 3 months you get meals, trips, dancing, and good sex.

If you start calling each other boyfriend and girlfriend you become creatures of habit sex gets slow the man don't try hard to please you like he did when they meet you the phone conversations get dry you lie or make up stuff to keep a conversation going she said.

So she only date's for a period of five to six months.

Christina thought to herself I never had that happen to me but I've only been with two men and after a two year relationship both were still pumping strong at least 3 nights a week when time allowed because each of us had very busy schedules.

Wait Tonya might be right she said with a frown on her face.

Being very busy is the reason both of my relationships broke up.

Hum it may be something to my girl's theory she said with a lifted eyebrow.

Tonya is a very sexual person and three days a week is just crazy to her and it might be months in between oh hell no she always had a guy who she always could call but she would never make him her man, all of those months in the hospital I know she's in need I feel sorry for the person she beds down.

Tonya headed to the bedroom to grab her cell phone before Mylz got there.

BAM!

Tonya noticed her window open next to her bed how did that get open she said with a frown on her face.

Did I open it she questioned?

Well my sweetie is on his way let me get ready she went to the closet and opened the double doors.

She Screamed! Help, Help!

A tall dark man was standing their inside he jumped out and grabbed her. He looked familiar she thought as she tried to fight stop it bitch he whispered in her ear he had his hand over her mouth and the other on her neck.

Tonya was pulling at his arms trying to break his tight grip around her neck.

His hand came off her mouth real quick and he punched her in the eye be still.

Tonya tried to scream but he hit her again. Not again she thought Jesus not again fight she told herself.

The man then pushed her on the bed and he was on top of her.

If you make a sound I'll kill you for sure this time he said. His eyes were red like fire his breath was hot as steam anger was all over him. How can I calm him she thought? Relax she told herself.

I hate you for living I tried to kill your ass and you survived Realtors or whores I'll kill all of you Bitches before I'm finished.

Tonya knew it was no calming this guy.

Smack he punched Tonya in the face and tightened his grip on her neck.

Tonya struggled to get free she felt sweat beading up on her forehead her air was weak she scratched and pulled at his arms and face he would not let go.

Ring, Ring, Ring.

Tonya. She heard a voice say.

Tonya woke up she was on the floor in her bedroom sweat was all over her face and body her clothes were soaked and wet. She had passed out Tonya she heard a voice coming from the front door.

Tonya got up slow and walked slowly to the front door and opened it.

She fell right into Mylz arms.

Mylz rushed to catch her Tonya he yelled are you all right!

He grabbed her and then he looked around the entryway, of her house with a shocked look on his face.

What happened Tonya? Who? Is anyone here? Tonya! Tonya! He yelled.

Mylz brought her into the living room and placed her on the couch.

He went into the kitchen to get a towel and wet it for her head.

Tonya, Mylz said as he tapped her on the side of her face.

Yes Tonya said slowly as she opened her eyes what happened, Tonya asked unaware of the black out.

He's here she shouted! He's here!

Mylz jumped who's here he said as he looked around the room.

Tonya reached for her neck rubbing it softly he's here my room in the closet he tried to me kill me again.

She was scared sweat beading up on her nose, her eyes were glossy she trembled he's here she repeated shaking her head side to side.

Mylz got up I'll look for him where is the bedroom?

No! Don't leave me please!

Well I need to check your house.

Take me with you.

Mylz and Tonya went from room to room the house was empty and all the windows were closed and locked.

Tonya tell, me what happened. Mylz asked nicely.

Tonya sat on the couch puzzled.

She said quietly, after we talked I walked into the bedroom the window was open and a man was in the closet he jumped me he choked me her tone quickened he punched me in the face he was choking me he wanted to kill me he was here she said as she cried.

Mylz put his arm around Tonya she laid her head on his shoulder there's no one here I think you may have had a dream.

Did you lie down after we spoke?

Tonya raised her head quickly and looked at Mylz. No.

Tonya placed both hands over her face she had realized that she got up off the floor when she heard him calling her name.

Oh my god she thought to herself I must have blacked out I don't want to tell him that she said to herself.

Mylz it must have been a dream I'm sorry I scared you.

Excuse me she said as she got up and left the room.

Mylz wanted to help but he had no idea what just had happened let me go get my bag out of the car and give you a look see, just to make me feel better he told himself.

Tonya came back a few minutes later to see Mylz with her medicine and his bag what is that black bag for Dr. She asked playfully.

I wanted to check you out if you don't mind miss.

I'm fine forget about it she walked over and sat by him so this is my med's she asked.

Yes he said looking in to her beautiful face

Mylz forgot all about being the Dr. and checking her out.

This is for pain and this one is for swelling.

The instructions are on the bottles take as needed he said staring at her.

Mr. Mylz you are so fine she said to herself Tonya had a habit of talking to herself.

His eyes are so glossy wet, his skin Carmel and smooth, lips just to die for, teeth white as snow damm she thought.

My man she thought, smart and fine mama would love for me to keep this one.

Tonya could not take her eyes off him.

Well Mylz said in an unsure tone I see your looking better I should be going I don't want to disturb you. So I'll get out of your way he replied.

Oh, Okay Tonya said so fast that she wished she didn't.

Why did you say that girl she asked her self I swear she said to herself.

You know that he is not in the way with his fine ass self.

I hope you don't have to go back to the hospital.

No I'm off. I'm going home to get some well-deserved rest.

Are you working tomorrow?

No as a matter of fact I'm not.

That's nice Tonya said smiling.

What do you do when you're not working? If you don't mind me asking

You can ask me anything. Mylz said to himself.

No I don't mind. I play a little gulf or go to the gym, do a little reading, or go for a bike ride at the beach.

I try to get out and enjoy my days off which are few.

I didn't hear anything about any dating, dining or visiting a woman that's cool she said to herself as a big smile came across her face.

No social life she asked

I thought I told you that I was single in the hospital.

I haven't had that for a while now.

Tonya thought to herself I hope you are not one of those fine ass down low brothers.

Stop tripping she said to herself, you know this man wants you.

I haven't met the right woman yet so I concentrate on my work but things are looking up he said smiling looking into Tonya's face.

Smiling back she said to herself I hope you're talking about me.

O Yeah she said as she lick her lips.

Well let me go Mylz said again I'd be here talking forever.

Oh no you want Tonya thought.

Just as it was getting good she thought.

Thank you again Dr Freeman for bring me my medicine and catching my fall, I'm so sorry for scaring you with my nightmare, she said with a little laugh.

I would love it if you call me Mylz.

I'm off work remember?

Sorry. Tonya said with her head tilted and a smirk on her face.

Mylz it is.

Mylz took Tonya hand and asked are you sure you're all right looking straight into her eyes like he was going to kiss with everything in him.

Tonya felt wet yes I'm all right it must have been a dream.

I'm really sorry for that. She said filling a little embarrassed.

May I call you later and check on you Mylz asked with concern in his voice

Sure that would be fine.

After her good byes to Mylz Tonya closed the door, turned and leaned back against it feeling a little confused about her earlier incident. What the hell had happen she thought?

Ring! Ring.

Hello.
He was just there for the homecoming party
Mylz! Girl he is so handsome oh, I just want him.
Well why didn't you get him?
I can't believe I fainted right in front of him.

Tonya said really fast every time she was excited she would talk 10miles an hour.

Tonya calm down Christina yelled into the phone.
What was he doing at your house?
Christina was worried.
Fainted what, what do you mean fainted?
He wasn't doing what I needed him to be doing.
Tonya your ass is nasty.
Tell me you did not faint for real.
Girl I did Tonya said slowly.
Mylz brought me my medicine, and yes I did faint.
Girl something is wrong with my head.
Tonya had no idea what was in store for her.
Oh I see Christina said he made a house call just to bring your medicine. Right.

Girl its true he brought me my meds and he caught my fall as soon as I open the door.
If anything would have happen between us you would have been the second one to know.
I would have been the first.

Tell me what happen with the fall Christina asked?

All I remember was Mylz calling me through the front door I thought I was dreaming.

I picked myself up off the hallway floor and headed to the door and when I reach for the door and open it apparently I fainted right in his arms.

The next thing I saw was Mylz looking down at me I was on the couch and he was sitting by me.

Christina laugh a little what do you mean that you picked yourself up off the floor?

Tonya laugh two, yes you know how I hate to fall more than anything in the world.

Just the vision made Christina laugh again.

No for real it's not funny I didn't fall or trip I think I would have remember that I really don't know how I got down on the floor.

One minute I was leaven the liven room to get cute for Mylz and the next minute he was at the door calling my name.

I never even heard the doorbell ring.

Christina started laughing loud wait, wait start all over tell me exactly what happen before I pee on myself laugh Christina as she held her stomach with one hand and the phone with the other.

Okay bitch quit laughing this is for real I m tripping on this.

I'm, I'm sorry Christina said through her laughing I just know that you hate to fall and it's too funny to think that you of all people fell.

Listen Tonya said try to make all of this make since.

I was talking to Mylz about 5pm than we hung up; I said to myself it will take him a few minutes to get from the hospital to my house so I'll go freshen up.

Tonya had lots of confusion in her voice.

Christina knows now that she was scared.

Girl I turned to walk to the bedroom and when I heard Mylz calling me from the front door I think I got up from the floor yes I'm pretty sure I did get up from the floor.

The next thing I remember is him looking down at me and I'm lying on the couch.

I glanced at the clock it was 6:00pm.

And I was dressed in the same dame shit.

My face was sweating my neck was wet Mylz got a wet cloth and put on my head.

Christina sat down in the chair this was serious I'm sorry I was laughing girl this is not right she said as she took a drink of her coffee.

Girl what if it was someone else at the door, you are lucky it was Mylz at the door.

Christina, Mylz also said that I was yelling he's here, he's here.

Mylz and I went all around the house checking for a burglar.

Tonya your scaring me now are you sure that no one was in your house?

I don't even know Tonya said in a low tone.

Who do you think was in your house Christina asked with real concern nothing was at the least bit funny at this point.

Chills ran through her body as Tonya went on.

Girl I played that shit off I told the Dr. I might have been having a nightmare or something, I told him that I was lying across the bed before he arrived.

What did he say? I need to go back and have another checkup.

Bullshit Tonya said I just got out of the hospital.

I think the party and the being home has over whelmed me and if you think for a minute I'm going back to the hospital your ass is crazy.

I'm cool trust me.

Girl; don't let me call Dr. Mylz myself, I'll do it and you know I will.

I wish I could erase everything that happen to you if I could I would.

You really need to be careful and make an appointment if this happen again.

I will I promise Tonya said just to make Christina feel better.

She knows that Christina would bug her about this for the next three hours if she did not agree.

Hay hold on girl my other line is ringing.

Click, Christina switch lines.

Hay baby what's up?

You Christina said with a hint of passion in her voice, and a big smile on her face.

By his smooth sound in his voice she could tell that he was lying down, oh how I wish I were lying on top of him she thought to herself.

Tonya was weighing heavy on her mind right now.

Baby hold on, before Kenny could respond he was already switched.

Kenny laid there on his back thinking of his beautiful woman, Damm he said to himself this woman has really got my nose open he remembered his single life and how he thought then life was perfect.

No weight, no pressure, no responsibility of another person calling him needing and wanting his time. I thought that life was what I wanted.

Just myself and my work. Which worked for years, a man was not meant to be along I now realize that.

With Christina in my life I don't want to be without her, I don't want no one else loving her or me.

When I think about her I smile, when I'm away from her I miss her, when we are together I feel complete

Man Kenny said to himself what are you doing? You sound as if you are in love he said with surprise in his voice.

Kenny got off the bed and looked at himself in the mirror; he saw a very happy and handsome man that deserves to be in love.

He looked hard at himself and liked what he saw.

He stood there no shirt on only a pair of black shorts on the image of a black king he said, and I'm in love with a black queen.

Kenny thought to himself as baby face played on the cd player in the other room I only think of you on two occasions that's day and night that was exactly how he felt about his girl.

Hello, Hello Christina said quickly.

Hello my beautiful queen Kenny said with a powerful new tone in his voice.

He realized that Christina is his queen and he's her king she has always treated him wonderful almost better than he has treated himself and that felt really good.

He remembered after he first kissed her she was the only thing he could think about, he then realized just what his life was missing.

One thing his mother would always say to him is baby kisses don't lie.

A kiss tells more than you know, it speaks volume it tell things that words can't say.

Especially early on in a relationship, a kiss is silent talking Kenny thought to himself.

Sweet heart I'm sorry I put you on hold so long that was Tonya on the other line.

Is she ok? He asked really concerned about their friend.

Tonya she is going through something I think she had a black out today maybe it was to early for her to come home.

Maybe it was the surprise party and the dancing she was doing these last few days, it could be that she needs more rest.

Kenny said all of that may have been too soon and it could have been to over whelming.

I just think she might need to have another checkup or something, I don't feel good about this.

She passed out in the bedroom Dr. Freeman called her and told her he would bring her the medicine that she needs.

Tonya said that she got up from the floor to answer the door and when she opened the door she passed out again right into his arms.

What kind of shit is that? Christina said as she hunched her shoulders.

Wait! Wait Kenny said when did Dr. Freeman start making house calls?

That's what I said to Christina smiled, but I'm glad he was there when she answered the door and not someone else.

But that's another story she said quickly.

Baby she said that she was out on the floor until she heard Dr. Mylz call her name through the door he had rang the doorbell a few times before he called her name.

Wait, Kenny said this guy drove all the way from the Hospital that's about 30 to 40 minutes.

So you mean to tell me from the time she hung up the phone and walked away the next minute she remembers was the Doc calling her from the door?

Yes that's what she said.

Damm Kenny replied.

Your girl had to be out 20 to 25 minutes that's not good

That's dangerous did she tell him?

And wait, she said when she woke up she was soak and wet.

Tonya answered the door and fainted right in Dr. Freeman arms.

What!

He looked her over and said she was all right.

I don't think so I think that she was just telling you that.

Kenny I think I need to spend the night over Tonya's house.

Kenny agreed but he really wanted Christina over his house in his arms in his bed.

The line got silent.

Kenny are you all right? Christina asked.

I'm just lonely, horny, and missing your body next to mine, all these thought went through his head all at once.

Baby I'm fine. I'm missing you.

But you're right, go see Tonya tonight just be careful and call me back tonight okay.

I tell you what I'll come by after I see Tonya, I'll just go by and check on her to see for myself that she's all right I want stay.

So keep all those thought because I'm missing you as well.

Christina said seductively.

Kenny did miss her he planed this quit evening a week ago.

We had been working so hard it was little time for each other in the past few weeks.

How did you know what I was thinking?

Hi sweetheart yes Christina said all is well Tonya is feeling a lot better.

I'm on my way.

Christina stared into Kenny's faced as he looked back at her that was their connection

Their body began to move together as if they were dancing to one of the favorite love songs.

She moved he moved the feeling was amazing he bent slowly down kissing her lips Christina eyes closed, Open your eyes baby she heard him say softly as he looked at her.

Christina body was pulsing she had reached climax she murmured and Kenny new it was time for him to release, his body moved a little faster Christina legs rapped around him she open up a little more he could feel the heat his body tighten and his eyes closed

And it happen open your eyes he heard her say slowly he open them and saw his beautiful woman. Damm girl was all he could say.

Kenny's was not finished he turned over as he pulled Christina beautiful body on top of his.

Christina kissed his neck and made her way to his nipples and began to tease one with her lips.

A smile appeared on his face.

Christina looked up in time to see Kenny's eyes closed and the big smile on his face.

Do you like that baby she asked? Yeah he said as he placed his hand in the small of her back and pulled her closer to him.

Tonya thought about something that her mom always taught her, nothing is possible; something is possible, anything is possible. Mom would say lots of people think nothing is possible because they don't think in terms of possibility. I feel that all is well in my life.

Tonya stood in her liven room looking at her mother beautiful picture that sits in a gold frame on the wall.

Wow!! A serious moment shake it off girl, she told herself. Ok, ok, ok Tonya said shaking her head.

Tonya walked over to the CD player and turned on her new Mariah Carry CD

She here her say touch my body and start dancing that's the jam Tonya said out loud.

As she danced around she noticed a book on her end table, who put this there?

Picking it up and reading the cover Finding Freedom She raised her eye brow thinking this sound familiar, By Jarvis Masters you're kidding she said out loud.

Tonya turned the book around and there was a picture of her favorite cousin Jay, what the hell he did it the boy is bad.

Mom must have dropped this off before she left yesterday.

Jay is her cousin on her mother side a good boy gone bad and now good again. I remember seeing him at the prison the week end just before my accident we discussed the possibility of his writing get published and now look at this.

Tony kissed his picture on the back cover.

Wow thinking back when she and her cousin would get together those was the days.

Jay was all was adventuress he thought he was James Bond; he was a brave little boy.

Always with a story of something he had done, when we got together we would say Jay tell us a story?

Ok he would say remember when thats how every story started.

When we heard remember when we know that we were in for a great story.

He told me and his younger sister Carla who is another of my favorite cousin how he got his first peace of sex.

My aunt Cindy was a wild beautiful woman who could get any and every thing she wanted.

A Brick house, when that song came out we know that that group was talking about Auntie Cindy.

Auntie was out there in the streets it was many times my mom would have to go and get all of my cousins because auntie would leave them home alone, her neighbors would call the police on her.

Jay told us how auntie brought two of her girlfriends home and a couple of men home and they were all getting drunk and popping pills.

Jay saw that one of the ladies had some dollars hanging out of her bra we started laughing so hard.

He waited for about two hours in his bedroom which was a few steps from the liven room he could see that the liquor was taking its toll along with the pills every one fell asleep.

Jay said he snuck in real quiet tip toeing across the room ducking behind an oversize chair that was in auntie's liven room rolling on the floor doing all of his James Bond move's on a mission he said

While on the floor he rose up and picked at the lady face making sure she was knocked out.

He then notice that the money was still sticking out of her bra and the way she was spreaded out on the couch he could see she had no panties on under her skirt.

Laughing hard, Carla and I said go on tell the story.

Stop laughing he said.

Jay could hardly tell the story because he was laughing too.

I just pulled it up and laid on her and started humping on her really fast and than I would drop on the floor just in case she wake up, man I did this about five times than my thang started feeling funny and then my pants got wet I got off he said smiling.

You are nasty Carla said I just laugh and laugh.

After I robbed her I robbed one of the dudes too just because, that started me on the path of robbery and sex.

That boy is a fool Tonya remembered.

Tonya and Carla goes to see Jay at least Three times a year, seeing Jay to me is like Christmas because you will always get a happy feeling from him, he's a present in himself I feel joy even when I receive a letter from him, he's so creative so positive he see's the good in every bad situation I just love being around him she thought.

I use to wish he was my brother because he was always doing crazy stuff.

Wow! Now look at this he has a published book out amazing.

Today started like any other day I was sitting at the coffee shop on Fredrick street I saw many cars passing by and people going in and out of the stores that were near by, I sat drinking my coffee just wanting to be alone in the peace of the beautiful morning that I had the pleasure of being in.

This morning at the gym was great all of the regulars were there as usual, I love the front desk girls especially Audra she's the best she is a young black girl about twenty years old pretty round face with medium black hair thick body, All ways greeting people with a big bright smile. This

Monday morning Audra was a little upset I asked were is that beautiful smile I'm used to seeing? She told me about this older white woman who was so upset that Audra opened the gym five minutes late she had Audra heated. The gym opened at Four thirty in the morning, Audra arrived at Four thirty three and the woman went off.

Catherine is the bitch name she's someone who wakes up mad and goes to sleep mad. Today she was complaining that those three minute was going to set her whole work out off track she went on telling Audra that she is not doing her job right she should know by now that four thirty means four thirty not four thirty three. And she has been working out here for the last three years and the last front desk girl that opens up the gym late was fired because she had called cooperate office on her. Like she was bragging or something.

John a regular gym member that was standing behind her said lady just check in and leave this girl alone. I need her to know how I feel she said to John with her face all balled up and her eyebrows raised, go on and get out of my way John told her because if you were in my face like that I would have slapped your ass long time ago.

Audra looked at him, smiled, and winked and he winked back.

The other members piled in from the parking lot and went to do what they do.

Hi Christina, hey mom, how are you?, baby I'm a little scared, I was trying to reach Tonya.

I spoke with her this morning I called her about seven this morning she was home Christina said.

I just called the house and sweetie she did not answer.

I think she had appointments this morning after she went to the gym.

Baby I think your right she might be at that gym lord I hope she don't over do it.

So how is my boyfriend Kenny, mom asked playfully.

Mom Kenny is well he is in New York visiting friends at his old job. Christina said sadly.

How long will he be gone?

Just for two days.

How is pop doing? Christina asked trying to change the subject.

Great! Things are well over here now that Tonya is so much better pop can finally concentrate on work again.

Well sweetie I am going to let you go now and I will call Tonya I guess later, by baby.

By mom, Christina said.

This coffee taste so good Tonya said to herself,

What? Tonya said as she looked behind her.

She turns looking around but there was no one there.

Shit, I heard his voice; my mind is playing tricks on me.

With this passing out shit, my mind was as tricky as a magic act.

Breathe girl breath I told myself.

I need to stay calm, slow in and slow out I said as I took long breath's in and out.

I hear him over and over again you have a small tumor on your brain that is causing these black out's. Dr Mylz said to me.

I went to the Hospital yesterday just for a check up and to see my handsome Dr.

I went through all these test and all the poking and given all the blood that I had left in me

Just to see this fine ass man.

I would have never guessed that my fainting spell was something so serious; I thought that I was just doing a little much as always.

After the entire test was complete, I got dressed and meet Dr. Freeman in his office.

Hey, he said as he entered the office holding all the test results.

I started smiling and said hey back to him in a very flirty way.

Mylz sat down with a serious look on his face as he looked over my tests.

What's up I asked with concern.

He looked up and stared directly in to my eyes.

By the way he raised up and took in a deep breath staring at me I know

I did not want to here the words that was about to come out of his mouth.

Kenny how are thing in New York?

It's great baby I got you something last night when I was out with the guys. Kenny said proudly.

What! What did you get me? Christina said with excitement.

I'll show you tomorrow when I get back.

Do you need me to pick you up from the airport?

No I arranged for a car to pick me up I will meet you at your job about Ten Thirty in the morning.

Ok sweetheart I miss you, Christina told Kenny in a way that only he and she knew.

Baby don't talk to me like that you know what happens when you talk in that voice

Yeah I know I really know.

I want to feel you right now all over me. Christina said smiling she know just how to turn Kenny on.

Baby, Baby please do not do me like that I'm on my way home in the morning hold up alright.

Kenny breathing was rapped she could tell that she was pushing his blood to all the right spots.

Christina remembered the one thing Kenny did that was so great is that Kenny really knows how to make love to her.

Kenny always seem to love her like he would never see her again it was very scary and at the same time so special.

Sweetheart listen Mylz said softly, I see some things on the x-rays that do not look good I need to check you into the hospital right now.

What, what the hell are you talking about Tonya yelled as she stood up and walked over to Mylz.

I just wanted to run out of his office and out of the hospital.

What I see on the x-ray looks to be a small tumor on the side of your brain that's why you're passing out sweetheart.

You are kidding right. Tonya said with eyebrows raised, you are kidding.

Chills ran up Tonya's body slowly. In shock, Tonya turned away from Mylz.

I moved towards the door grabbing my purse I walked out and down the hall, my worst nightmare had come true something was wrong.

Shit I don't believe this; my family can't take any more bad news.

Suddenly I felt tension and tightness take over my body I need some air I thought to myself I walked faster and faster towards the automatic doors just as I went through the air slapped me so hard in the face as if it was trying to snap me back to reality.

Tears were starting to run down my cheek's how could this be happening? The tears came faster and my heart was pounding fast it felt like the world could see each beat.

I looked around to see if anyone was looking at me I felt lost I need someone to find me.

I stop walking and just held myself; suddenly I felt another pair of arms holding me too.

Layers and layers of bad news brought me back to the first day I woke up and seen all my family looking down at me with tears in their eyes

That freaken bastard I said by this time I was in full crying mold, shaking and sniffing, straight feeling sorry for myself.

I have to get away from here I don't want to believe this.

Tonya thought to herself.

Mylz placed my head on his chest as the tears ran faster as he and I stood out in front of the hospital.

I'll be alright I said as I looked up into Mylz face, I wiped fresh tears from my eyes I will be all right?

Do you need me to get you anything Mylz asked softly?

Yes I said inside myself get me the F—away from here this cannot be for real.

No I mean yes some water

I really need some water please.

I need some medicine she thought as she looked through her purse.

Tonya entered the lobby looking for a place to sit; her head was hurting now, what a beautiful place this is she thought as she looked around the hospital.

The decoration was certainly expensive and upper class and it shows, beautiful bright colors cheerful pictures and some of the best and worse news come out of these walls.

Mylz returned with the water sat down beside her and gave her the water putting his arms around her and held Tonya tight.

I just want to a sure you that I will do everything in my power to make you better, your in good hands Mylz said in a soft sexy tone that would make any sick woman well in a hurry.

Shit I know she thought as she could feel Mylz powerful strong arms still around her just holding her close.

I just need to get some air and think Tonya said as she got up and headed for the door.

If I get out of here, she thought to herself I am not coming back so he can for get that shit in a real way.

Mylz grabbed Tonya, wait lets talk, Tonya stared into his eyes for few seconds turned and walked off trying not to let the tears fall from her eyes.

When I finally reach the doors, they opened after walking out my tears fell fast I was so scared that I started trembling. I found myself wondering how I can tell my parents this news. I can't even tell Christina, or Milo Damm.

It was time to take a stand and figure out what I need to do.

This news was more than I expected. Myz stepped out of the doors of the hospital I can see that he was concerned and it seem serious.

Tonya I really think that we need go think about calling your family and let them know because we need to check you in and get you set up

Hold up set up for what Tonya said with a lot of emotion. Do you really think that I'm checking myself back into this hospital?

Yes Mylz said seriously.

No I'm not Tonya said with attitude.

Ring

Ring, Tonya looks at Mylz and then at her cell it's her mom. Damm she thought I cannot handle this right now she can always tell when I'v been crying.

I must look a mess she thought.

I need to go to the woman's room I'll be right back

Mylz was still standing in the lobby,

Christina walked in.

Good morning Dr Freeman how are you Christina said cheerfully.

Mylz looked as if he had seen a ghost.

With raised eyebrows, what did I say she said?

Good Morning Christina and how you, Mylz said in a very worried tone.

Mylz was worried that Tonya would come out of the women room and see her.

No I just was thinking.

How are you doing this morning? Mylz asked trying to sound more alive.

Great Christina said.

How is Kenny?

All is well Christina said smiling he will be back from New York this morning and I cannot

Wait to see him.

Wow! New York at this time of year must be nice Myz thought.

Hey I have to run I'll talk to you later Christina said with a rush in her voice.

Yeah yeah I'll talk to you later have a great day Mylz said as she walked toward the

Elevator

Ring. Ring Damm why is she calling me back to back is something wrong with dad.

Trying to stop sniffing and get herself together Tonya answers.

Hello.

Hey sweetheart where are you? I've been trying to call you all morning are you at that gym place?

Did you get my message this morning; have you been back to your house?

Mom was shooting questions thirty miles an hour. Tonya just leaned up against the

Bathroom wall as she stared into the mirror.

Trying to sound calm Tonya tried to answer all of the questions that her mom asked.

While the news that she just heard keep hitting her like a prize fighter trying to get his

Last, knock out.

Mom I'm

Tonya got quiet while she began to wipe the fresh tears from her eyes, mom I'm.

Baby what's wrong? She shouted into the phone.

Mom, mom, Tonya said through her tears.

Tonya are you crying?

Where are you?

I'll come there where are you?

I'm at the hospital but mom she said wiping her cheeks and eyes she paused for a

Moment while she was trying to pull herself together because she knows how her mom worries.

What! What happen is everything ok?

What hospital? When did you get there?

Did you get hurt?

Why are you crying?

The questions was hitting fast and hard so hard it made the tears run down her face faster pity was setting in and pain came over her whole body she was trembling again.

Stop crying she told herself.

Hi Kenny Kim said as he entered the lobby of Christina office.

Hi back to you Ms Kim Kenny said in a happy tone.

How are things with you?

All is well, thanks you for asking.

Where is my girl? Kenny asked

She's in there Kim said as she pointed to Christina office, I think she on a conference call

With all the hospital directors.

I'll just pop my head in and let her know that I'm here.

Kenny open the door after a few taps on it, stuck his head in and winked at Christina.

Christina smiled and waved him in.

Yes John, Christina said if progress means lying to ourselves about the truth of human

Existence, than we must have a new criterion of progress.

Health care is already fast becoming a major economic indicator.

Yes your right Christina said, John you know I think things are just getting out of hand.

While aging, sickness, and death are inevitable, good quality health care plans are

Important.

Kenny waited in the set in front of Christina desk just admiring the way she know how to

Handle her business.

John I agree with you on one point—the main thing is that you are honest with your

People.

Christina wanted off the phone her man was back and she needed a big hug and a kiss.

Ok people lets go ahead and call this meeting over send me all of the updates on things

We need to implement into our new program ok.

Thank you all Christina said in her professional voice and we will talk again next week.

Christina hung up the phone.

Hey sweetheart how was your flight?

Kenny walked over to Christina side of the desk, placed his arms around her waist.

The flight was great now where is my kiss?

Christina looked up at her handsome man and relaxed in his arms as they kissed.

Tonya walked out of the bathroom and into the lobby,

Mylz was waiting she handed him her phone. And took a seat with her back turned from everyone.

No one behind her could tell she was crying

During Tonya's life she could never imagine that she would get a ticket like this, all kind

Of medical problems, man what a difference a day make she thought to herself as

She fought back the tears.

Tonya wanted to make sense of it; I have always been such a nice. Caring, given

Person how she asked how can this happen.

At first this new information about my life was frightening. Now I just

Want to pretend that I'm just sleeping; I'm in my bed just sleeping.

This news has me so shaken it plays like a movie in my mind how on earth could this

Be happening to me?

Tonya sat in the chair next to the window with her back turned away from every body.

Mylz was still on the line with Tonya's mother.

Baby Mrs. Gardener said to her husband Tonya is at the hospital. Before she could get

Anything else out of her mouth Mr. Gardener took the phone out of her hands.

Hello, Hello Mr. Gardener said quickly.

Hello Dr. Freeman said how are you sir?

I'm fine is this Dr. Freeman Mr. Gardener said surprisingly yes sir it is.

What's going on man?

Well Tonya is here with me at the hospital and we just completed a few test.

What kind of test Mr. Gardener said loudly into the phone.

Sir wait a minute I can explain it all to you let me go to my office right now we are on

Tonya's cell and I don't have the ex-rays in front of me I'll call you right back.

What is my daughter alright? I'll call you right back

Mylz hung up the phone and gave it back to Tonya lets go to my office and get out of the lobby he said in a soft voice.

Tonya could only imagine what the rest of this day would be like.

As Dr. Freeman enters his office he realized that all he wanted to do is put his arms around Tonya and make everything better.

What did my Mother say? She asked with concern.

It was your dad that I was speaking to he said without looking at her.

My dad! What is he doing home at this time of day?

I told them that I would call them back as soon as I got in my office.

Have a seat sweetheart; I need to know what we are going to do about this information.

Mylz asked.

Before. I call your parents back just how much do you want me to tell them if anything.

You know I can do that Tonya Said in a low tone it's my job to let them know.

She know that had to be the case she did not want Dr. Freeman blowing things up and having her parents loosing a another night rest behind her.

Tonya decided to soften things up a bit just telling a half truth.

I will do it she said with confidents.

At that moment, she discovered that if she wanted to make it through this she needed to get tough.

Desperate to get out of the hospital Tonya told Dr. Freeman that she would go right over to her parents and tell them what's going on.

Dr. Freeman made a quick call to the Gardeners. Mr. Gardener answered the phone.

Mr. Gardener this is Dr. Freeman calling you back Tonya just left my office she is coming over to talk with you and your wife about what's going on.

I have to go now I was just calling back like I said I would see you soon.

An eerie feeling passed over Tonya how was she going to tell her parents this.

Tonya throat clogged with emotions.

This just has to be all right, I need them to take this information well. Tonya wants to just forget the helplessness she felt today after she got the news from Mylz.

She hit the window's power button, opening the window so the fresh air could hit her face.

Dr Walker Mylz said smiling as he stood up to shake his hand.

How are you today man, I'm good what up buddy?

Mylz and Dr. John Walker has been friends sense their college days

Man its great to see you hey do me a favor while you're here.

I need you to look over these x-rays and give me your thoughts.

Mylz placed the x-rays on the board and turn on the light behind it.

Mylz stomach tightens as he looked at the x-rays.

Dude who does these belong too, and where is this person right know John said with concern in his voice.

Mylz rubbed his hand over his face, these are Tonya's.

Not your Tonya John asked with a look of surprise.

John was the only one Mylz told about his crush on Tonya John new how Mylz felt about this woman.

He was glad that his best friend finally notices that being alone was not good for him.

Damm. Now the first woman he found was going through so much, when did you do these x-rays man?

Did you tell her yet?

Yes man I had to, she been here all morning crying her eye's out.

Damm. Man John said softly.

Listen man this is fixable. That's the great thing about it.

John is Mylz best friend a very handsome man six feet three about two hundred twenty pound very athletic a ladies man for sure Carmel brown skin with light soft brown eyes that always look as if they are shining with straight white teeth and short wavy black hair.

John has always had a big effect on the ladies even in college, one thing that Mylz respect about his friend is that John is a very professional man when it comes to business there are certain lines he refuses to cross like dating people he work with.

In our profession we meet lots of women and work around lots.

Mylz man this need to be attended to right away man get her back here and we can take it from there.

John walked around Mylz desk and placed his hand on his shoulder, man it's going to be alright.

Just as John finished his sentence, Christina walked in.

What's up girl? John said to Christina.

Hey John what's new with you? Nothing—same O same O.

It's been awhile, where have you been hiding Christina asked with excitement.

John and Christina was long time buddies every sense High School.

Well young lady I've been over seas teaching medicine for the last year but I'm back now.

Wow! How exciting Christina said.

How's life here? John asked

Its great things are looking up it was touch and go for a while with my best friend.

Now that she's better I feel good.

John and Mylz look at each other John hunched his shoulders.

I'm not taking work home any more. Christina said.

What! John said with his eye brows raised.

John looked over at Mylz man call the police I think someone is impersonating my girl.

Shut up I'm for real I have something else I mean someone else that's taking all of my free time.

You mean your dating.

Yes I am. Thank you very much.

Man call 911 right now I know this not my Christina. John said laughing.

What's so funny but head. Christina said in a playful manner

You are, John said you know that I was trying to get that stuff for the last Ten years.

You're full of shit Christina said laughing, you couldn't handle me even with back up.

That's my shit talking girl there John said with excitement in his voice.

Mylz jumped in you to are definitely back together again.

Christina walked over and put her arms around John,

Damm I sure have missed you, you have to meet Kenny.

Oh so that the joker's name.

Stop playing Christina said you will love him he just like your crazy ass.

But does he look as good as I do?

Mylz Christina said John is back arrogant as ever.

Anyway I will see you all later, John call when you get a chance and yes before you ask the number is still the same.

Tonya drove towards her parents' house just as she got to the light beep beep she heard a horn.

Not wanting to be bothered Tonya did not look over.

Tonya almost knew everyone in town.

Bitch you know you hear me, the voice yell out.

Tonya thought to herself no the fuck this ass hole did not say that and who is he talking to?

Tonya looked straight ahead.

Beep Beep Bitch you know you hear me, she heard again.

This time she recognized the voice, Tonya smiled to herself.

It was Richard, Richard and Tonya, Christina John, Milo, Linda, Kim and the crew go back a long way

Richard a fine black man six Three caramel brown skin perfect white teeth slender face with very high cheek bones with beautiful hazel eyes, thin built brother with a big round butt, long legs a shape any woman would die for.

Richard is our gay friend and he's a great friend and story teller, if you want to laugh call

Richard over get some cocktails and a blanket and it's on.

Richard always had drama going on and he sure could take your mind off your troubles and sometimes help you out with them too.

Tonya put on her blinker to pull over she was very glad to see her friend.

Tonya got out of the car and Richard did too hey bitch Richard yell.

Tonya yell what's up whore Tonya and Richard hugged each other.

Oh, what is this Miss thang why are you out looking so tow up. Richard asked using his girly voice.

Tonya smiled to keep from crying all over again.

Thanks bitch glad you noticed, Tonya said smiling.

No for real Miss thang what's the hell going on who must we go fight now?

Richard said with his hand on his hip and eyebrows raised poking his lips shaking his head side to side.

Tonya stood there looking at her friend knowing that no matter what his ass was down for the get down.

Reflecting back about three years ago when Richard was involved with this married man named Smitty.

Smitty was a very sharp brother owner of a tire and wheel shop called the 959 he has nothing but bad boys around him all day long.

Smitty very business like we thought, actually he was nothing other than a down low brother wanting to get his freak on every chance he got.

A tall good looking light skin brother long good hair always wore it in a pony tail, a big football type man big muscles every wear, broad shoulders a man that look like he sure could protect a sister.

Smitty meet Richard when Richard went to get rims put on his 7 series BMW.

Richard could tell right away that Smitty was not the man he was made out to be.

Smitty was a pro at hiding his down low side if your not from there you would never know.

Richard know, Richard notice the way Smitty was watching him that he was interested in getting to know him better. Richard jumped at the opportunity to see just how far he would go after he made the initial contact.

Hello, my name is Richard, I have an appointment with Sal to get my rims put on my ride today, Richard said using his regular voice, staring him straight in his eyes right than Richard new that Smitty felt him.

Sal will be right out, what's your name Smitty asked again, Richard, No last name was given at that time I did not want to give him too much info right away Richard thought to himself.

Dress to the tee Richard stood tall wearing his straight leg jeans the ones that gave his butt just a little more rise, a pair of ill skin black boots, with a long sleeve black button down shirt with just enough buttons open for you to see his chest, with a black blazer.

Smitty stood there taking in Richards's beauty, it was always like that Richard looks got him a lot of attention from men and woman.

Smitty told me that it would take about three hours to do my ride, he than asked if I was going to wait in the lobby or did I need a ride home. The shop would call when the car was finished.

Richard want you fill this out for me and we'll get right to work.

Smitty handed me a work order form that needed all of my personal info.

Thanks man Smitty said.

I filled it out and handed it back to him.

You know I think that I'll go over to that Star buck's and grab a latté and do some work.

Richard turn and walked towards his ride he could feel Smitty watching him.

Grabbing his brief case out of the car Richard turned to go back in the shop to return his car keys, to his surprise Smitty was right behind him.

Startled Richard jumped sorry man Smitty said.

I just came out to get the keys.

Handing the keys to him, I stepped back.

So this is your cell number right? Smitty asked smiling.

Yes it is I'll just be right there you can see me if you look, Richard said in a flirty way.

Tonya girl what the hell's got into you? And where are you coming from?

Nothing, and I just left the hospital.

Well did your best friend die or what. Richard said as a joke.

Tonya felt just as if her best friend had died how could she tell her parents this news.

No butt head, I had a couple of fainting spells and I had a couple of test and the news is not the best news.

Oh Richard said as he put both hands over his mouth I know what's coming next Tonya thought to herself.

Richard solution to everything is get some dick and think about it later.

Girl you're kidding me how bad is it.

Dr. Thinks it's a small tumor and he want to operate right away or I will keep having these fucked up fainting spells.

Wow! Richard said surprisingly.

Well I excuse you for looking that way Richard said trying to lighten up the mood.

Well tell me this did you pass out while you were getting the dick?

Hell no Tonya said madly it been a long time since I even seen a dark bar and a bag of nuts.

Oh my bitch that's why you are passing out no kitty action.

Fuck you Richard Tonya said as she punched his arm.

Poor Kitty, Poor Kitty, we have to find you a victim right away.

You got to love him Tonya thought to herself.

Miss thang I thought you had your eyes on that DR.

I do I want him bad Tonya replied, He moves just a little too slow.

That can feel good if you know what I mean Richard smiling with his eyebrows raised and one hand over his mouth.

Well thank god you ran into me today because you need professional help you need a man eater on your team and I mean a man eater Richard said with two snaps.

Let's get you fucking to night.

I'll follow you home call mom and let her know that things are fine and you will come by later.

I have work to do Richard said.

Tonya and Richard Returned to their cars and Tonya headed towards her house.

Tonya pull out her cell connected the blue tooth to the car and headed home

Call mother she said as she pulled away from the curb.

Calling mother she heard the car say.

After a few minutes, her mother picked up.

Hello, she said softly. Tonya could see her face clearly, mom hi it's me.

Baby, are you ok she asked with concern.

Yes I'm fine I'm on my way home I have some things to take care of and I'll come by later.

But are.

That's all she heard her mom say. Tonya quickly hung up the phone.

No more questions not now she thought to herself.

Pulling into the driveway Tonya felt a sense of relief.

Richard pulled into the driveway right beside her.

Tonya opens the door, walks in throws her keys on the table.

Girl the house is still marvelous Richard said.

Now move it move we don't have much time, Richard hurrying Tonya out of the hallway and into the living room.

What's the Dr. Number?

Oh how I missed you baby, I'm glad your back.

I'm glad I'm back to.

What's new sweetheart Christina asked in between her kisses she was planting all over his face. The joy of having such a wonderful woman Kenny thought to himself.

Man what a difference a day make he said New York was great but I rather be here with you.

Christina figured since Kenny just got off a long flight he need to be put to sleep in the way only she know how.

Baby what you say if we grab some food and head to my house.

Kenny knows just what that was about.

His girl might be a professional at work but she could be pretty freeeeeeaky at the house.

I think I'm going to take the rest of the day off and cater to you how would like that? Christina asked seductively.

Oh Yeah Kenny said raising one eye brow; I'll wait for you out side.

Hey my car is in the lot right in front I'll be right out.

Back at the house Kenny and Christina finished off their food and headed for the shower.

Kenny opens the glass door to the shower and turned on the water after a few minutes he adjusted it to the perfect temperature.

Kenny slowly unbuttons the top button of his shirt just as Christina walked in, hey let me do that she said softly.

Christina moved closer to him and slipped her body between him and the sink that he was standing in front of.

One by one she unbuttons each button while kissing is chest just above his wife beater.

Oh how good that felt to him he started getting warm and his friend was waking up.

Christina stuck her hands into his arm sleeves and gave a little push Kenny shirt felled to the bathroom floor.

Slowly she reached for the bottom of Kenny's wife beater and raised it up; she was a little too short to raise it high enough to get over Kenny's head so he took it off quick.

Heat was beginning to take over Kenny's body as Christina grabbed Kenny's belt.

Kenny did not know if it was the steam from the hot water or the steam from him that had started fogging up the mirrors.

Baby Kenny said come on now.

Say it again she said.

Baby you know I can't take this.

Christina still took her time taking off the belt just as she got the belt loose his pants dropped to the floor.

Nice boxers Christina said as she kissed his stomach.

Kenny was in full flame his dark bar stood up so big you could hang your bath towel on it.

That's all Christina needed to see, she started taking off her clothes to.

Kenny stepped into the shower letting the nice warm water sooth his body.

Christina stepped into the shower, placed her arms around his neck, and kissed him slow.

She could feel his hardness up against her stomach.

Christina was missing Kenny and she was on fire slowly she dropped to her knees.

Baby she heard him say that feels so good, baby oh baby she could fell his body tighten up.

Christina placed her hands on his ass and pulled him in closer.

Not now baby not now she heard him say please wait, wait, wait.

Christina slowed the movement and let him get control.

Kenny was looking down at her as she looked up reaching for her hand he helps her up

Kissing her lips he felt his dark bar get harder and harder.

Kenny turned Christina around, and kissed the back of her neck, and pulled her close to his body she could fell his big dark bar in her back.

He held her in his arm like he was holding her for the last time, I Love he said in her ear.

Christina turned around Kenny grabbed her face and kissed her again.

Kenny stepped out of the shower and wrapped himself with one of Christina oversized towels and reached in the shower and lifted Christina right off her feet.

Placing her wet body on a towel he had placed on the bed he began sucking her full size breast and down her stomach and down to the good spot the wet spot.

Christina moan and moved slowly in circles she could feel pressure from each suck don't stop she said in a low voice don't stop.

Kenny loved it when she talked to him; stopping was not a part of his plan.

Kenny felt Christina move become faster and faster, he wanted this to last so he slowly moved himself up her body until she could feel his hardness up against her clit.

This made Christina jump her body was very sensitive and she was ready.

Kenny she said as she tried to breathe slowly Kenny grabbed one of her breast, licked the tip of it, and blew the cold air made her nipple stand at attention.

Kenny, don't stop he heard her say Kenny looked at Christina her eyes were closed she was moving and into what he was doing to her body.

His gaze stayed on her as he whispered softly in her ear that feels so good sweetheart.

For a moment time stood still Kenny and Christina just laid, there still right than life was good.

Christina was conscious of how great her body felt the heat the way she was breathing the light touching and the way Kenny made love to her.

Kenny really knows how to please her and he knows just how she liked it.

A delicate smile was on Christina face.

What exactly do you want from this Dr.

Richard asked as he spun around and faced her.

I want him I really want him.

I know he wants me to she said with confusion in her voice.

Tonya was really thinking about the news that she had got earlier that day.

Ok Richard replied what's his number we'll call him and invite him to dinner so you too can talk about your situation.

That sounds like a plan.

Tonya and Richard went to work on their plan.

Dr Freeman was having a hard time at work after finding out that Tonya needed to have this surgery.

He walked the hall of the hospital drop seeing his patients and doing follow up visits with old patients.

The day was getting late and Mylz had just two more patients to visit before he leaves for the day

Mylz enter his office and sat down took a long breath just than he took out his pager and check to see if Tonya had called even though he know he didn't hear it ring.

After a minute or two his cell phone rings yes he thought when he saw Tonya home number show up in his caller Id, he was glad she was calling and he know where she was.

I hope she all right he then thought.

Hello he said quickly.

Hey Tonya said in a soft voice I was wondering if you have time to stop by and see me later.

Are you all right?

Yes. Do u think you might have a little time this evening?

O Yeah he thought to himself.

You know my day is light and I should be leaving about six.

I just want to be clear on my condition before I go tell my family, Tonya said.

Ok that's good; I can stop by on my way home if that's ok.

That's fine Tonya said trying to hide the joy she felt.

See you than Tonya said.

Mylz felt heat coming from his body all I really want to do is wrap my arms around her and make everything all right.

It was about four fifteen and she still had to get things ready.

Ok miss thang we have less than two hours let's get moving.

Tonya and Richard went to the market to pick up everything that was needed to have a perfect night.

On the way back to Tonya house Richard said now what will you be wearing when your boyfriend get there.

He's not my boyfriend bitch.

Yes he is and you know it especially after tonight if he's not your ass need to step up your game. Richard went in and right to preparing the meal.

Tonya stepped in to the bath to relax while Richard started the dinner.

Man what a difference a day make she thought.

Richard yelled to Tonya where is the Season salt?

In the right side of the cabinet near the stove, I bet you did not even look for it.

I found it you hurry now I want everything to go as plan.

Tonya lay back in the water and took a breath.

So this is how it is Tonya said to herself.

Uncertain on how her family would take the news she had to tell them Tonya just wanted to get through this even and trust that things would work out.

Tonya stood up in the tub and turn on the shower to wash off the bubbles.

Reaching for the towel Tonya felt like she was going to faint again, quickly she grab the towel and wrapped it around her.

Tonya tried to scream but nothing would come out suddenly Richard heard a loud noise.

Miss thang, what the hell was that.

Miss thang did you hear me?

Richard got really scared; putting down the knife he was holding and headed for Tonya's room.

Knock, Knock Hey he yelled are you all right he asked.

Richard listens at the door waiting for Tonya to answer him.

Tapping on the door again he said Tonya are you still in the bath? What was that noise?

Tonya sighed deeply, Richard voice woke her blinking Tonya tried to bring herself back

Into focus.

Tonya are you ok what the hell was that noise.

Richard Tonya yelled softly just above a whisper.

Richard opens the door to Tonya's bed room.

Richard he heard her say, I'm here he said as he helped her up from the floor.

What the hell happen Richard asked with surprise in his voice.

Unable to answer Tonya just stared at him.

Tonya held on to Richard arm as he walked her to her bed and sat her down.

This is ridiculous what kind of shit is this; yeah you need to go back to the hospital

Richard said with concern.

I don't think you and the Dr will be doing anything tonight.

Tonya forced a smile I'll be just fine she said; get out of my room I'll be right out.

Richard walked out mumbling and headed back to the kitchen.

The nerve under her left eye began to tic Tonya stood up and walked back into the bathroom

To get dressed nothing was going to mess up this night.

Mylz walked into his office after making his rounds; all is well he thought to himself.

All he wanted to do is get to Tonya house and make sure his girl was all right.

He was glad that she wanted to meet him tonight after the news he had to tell her made him feel bad.

Mylz being such a serious and professional man he was not easily turned on by feminine lures, no matter how tempting but there was something about Tonya Gardener.

Richard oh my god it smells good in here Tonya said as she walked into the kitchen

You have out done yourself as usual.

I swear if you were into woman you would have already been my husband Tonya said as she placed a kiss on his face.

Richard laughed.

If I was into woman I would have took some when you passed out Tonya laugh aloud. Well I can say you still are the sexiest woman I know Richard said softly.

Thank you Tonya said.

You and Christina I sure can't forget my other girl Richard said you bitches are bad to the bone.

Mylz want be expecting all this I hope he's hungry

Tonya went to the liven room and turned on the music flipping through the CD rack looking for her Brian McKnight CD yeah here it is.

After placing it in the player Tonya walked over to the slide door and opens it to let the fresh air from outside in.

That sure feels good Richard said as he walked over to the sliding door that led out on to the hardwood deck.

Miss thang it really romantic out here I thank this is where you should serve dinner girl.

I think your right Tonya said.

Richard walked back in; let's get a drink are you ok?.

These things come and go.

Well let's get that taking care of so you can be around to see me get married Richard said looking at Tonya.

Bitch you are not getting married you are to selfish and you can't stand the same dick for too long.

That is not true Richard said well maybe a little truth.

How can you get married and you don't even have a man.

Well I just said I was thinking of getting married and that mean your ass still need to be around for it.

I will, Tonya said softly I will I promise.

Christina took a shower and decided to call and see what Tonya was up to.

Tonya and Richard was finishing off their cocktail while listing to Toni Braxton CD when the phone rang.

Hey girl what's up Christina said?

I'm good you would not even guess who's here with me.

Who, I know I know Christina said with excitement in her voice.

It's Mylz.

No but he is on his way.

What.

Yes he'll be here soon.

Girl Richard ass he's been here all day with me and he fixed one of his famous meals for

Mylz and I.

Put him on the phone Christina said.

Hey Miss thang Richard said in his crazy voice.

Where have you been?

I was in the bay area for the last few months taking care of some things you know what I mean he said as they both started laughing.

Where are you Richard asked? How's that fine man of yours?

I'm home right now and that fine man of mind is still in my bed trying to regroup as we speak. That's my girl you're so nasty Richard said in his Miss thang voice.

When are we all getting together and hang out like we use to Christina said?

Richard thought back on his day with Tonya he knows that Christina didn't know about Tonya new problem.

He was silent for too long Christina said what's the matter with skeptic in her voice.

Richard was so close to them they all know when the other one was going through something.

Hold up something is wrong Christina said.

Are you ok?

Girl I'm just fabulous Christina listen real close to his answer she know when he was telling the truth.

That mean something was wrong with Tonya.

What's wrong with my girl Christina asked in her serious voice?

Well well that was Richard something wrong alert.

She know that ever since they were kids, Richard would always say well well before he spilled the beans on people.

Something was wrong and it was serious.

Is that why Mylz is on his was over there she thought to herself she know about Tonya's fainting spell but that could not be it she told herself.

Richard you better tell me everything right now in a voice that reminded him of his mother.

Richard had a quick flash back when he was a small child and his cousins can in from Atlanta to visit for two weeks.

They were all in the den at his house watching TV and Ronnie was hungry so we all made a plan to go and steal food from the kitchen it would have been better just to go ask.

Man that was a bad idea.

All of the grown up's were in bed it was about Three in the morning we crept down the hall and in to the kitchen Ronnie, went for the fried chicken that was in the refrigerator.

I went for the peanut butter John was in the Captain Crunch cereal, Milo was in the cookies all of a sudden the cookie jar fell off the counter; it was so loud that everybody took off running back down the hallway heading for the Den.

Man what happen? All of our hearts were beating fast Richard heard his mom foot steeps coming down the hall everyone was holding in there laugh they know that they were in big trouble.

What is going on in there they heard her say.

Everyone had their face buried into their pillow laughing because Richard had a look of terror on his face.

Richard mom turned on the light in the kitchen, her big fat cookie jar was on the counter, and the top of it was smashed on the floor.

RICHARD she yelled get your butt in here.

Mom always would say you tell me right now what happen in a way that made you think your air supply was about to be cut off.

Just than Richard heard Christina say Richard are you still there?

Snap snap miss thang start talking Christina said.

Well Well.

Tonya heard him say well one to many times she turn and gave him the look everyone know what that look mean.

Don't Tonya said shaking her head with her finger to her lips.

Richard opens his eyes wide and hunched his shoulders shaking his head from side to side.

Tonya took the phone right out of his hands.

Hey girl what's up?

You tell me Christina said in her big sister voice.

Nothing Richard and I are just talking about him getting married. Richard looked over at her with his hand on his hip and lips poked out, one brow raised and shook his head.

Wow!! Are you kidding?

Girl didn't you tell Richard that Kenny's there.

Yes, right here still trying to regroup.

Your nasty hey call us back go on and kick it with your guy everything is good here.

I'll be trying to get some tonight too Tonya said laughing.

Tramp you're the nasty one Christina said.

I'm going to try very hard to be nasty tonight. It just might be my last Tonya thought just as sadness came over her.

I'm going back in to get another cocktail I'll talk to you later.

Pour me a drink Richard please I'm feeling a little down I hate it when I can't tell Christina my problems.

She's like mom they worry too much.

Right now feeling sorry for myself is not an option I have to get better and that's it bottom line.

Mylz sat at his desk finishing off a few things trying hard not to drift his mind was only on his beautiful girl Tonya.

Man he said to himself that's not my girl I sure wish she was. Tonight ill make sure she know that I'm not just her Dr I'm truly interested in.

Mylz looked at his watch and seen its 6; 15 pm wow! Let me get out of here.

Mylz walk over to the coat hanger behind his office door, took off his white lab jacket, hung it up, pulled his leather jacket off the hook, and put it on.

Mylz walked into his private bathroom and rinsed his face dried it off and looked into the mirror.

Thinking man go get her what's up? Just than he remembered let me brush my teeth I know she will bring a big smile to my face got to keep the teeth white and the breath fresh just in case.

Man I'm hungry I need to get something to eat before I get to Tonya's house; maybe she's hungry to he thought.

Mylz picked up the phone to call Tonya.

Tonya hey your phone is ringing Richard yelled.

Answer it please I'm in the rest room.

Damm I'm chilling and she want me to play house keeper and answer phones, cook, fix drinks, Richard said feeling a little tipsy.

Hello, Tonya Gardener home how can I help you?

Richard said being funny.

May I speak to Tonya?

Whom may I say is calling?

This is Dr Freeman.

Who shit Mylz heard the voice on the phone say just before he heard a loud laugh.

Opps. Girl this is your Dr on the line.

I thought it was Christina calling back and I was playing on the phone.

Give me that phone Tonya said as she snatch it from Richard get you something to eat and bring that high down Tonya whispered to Richard.

Hello.

Hello Mylz said.

Hey I'm a little hungry would you like me to bring you something?

Tonya eye's got big well there's food here you came eat here if that's ok with you.

A big smile came over Mylz face sure, if it's not a bother.

Wow! Mylz thought thanks Tonya that sound's great I'm on my way than.

Great Tonya said see you in a minute.

All right Tonya said Richard take your butt in the guest room after you eat my sweetheart is almost here and I don't want you in the way.

Ok I'm going I'm going but bitch you better handle your business.

I hope you don't chicken out, Richard whispered as he passed by Tonya.

The doorbell rang fifteen minutes later.

Hi Dr.

Hi Tonya how are you?

Wow! Something smells good what did you make.

Just a little soul food mac and cheese, meat loaf, collard greens and corn bread. We will be eating on the patio just to your right Tonya pointed.

Sounds great Mylz said.

Mylz stepped out on the patio and took in the beautiful view of the city.

Dr. Here you are Tonya said as she stepped out with a Mylz plate.

Thank you.

I'm really thankful for a home cooked meal that I didn't have to cook.

Tonya smiled. Enjoy she said as she sipped her cocktail and watch Mylz eat his meal.

Tonya looked beautiful she wore a short dress with a three inch high sandal shoe with a diamond toe ring on her Middle toe she was trying to taunt Dr Freeman and she could tell he was taking in every inch of her.

You look nice he said softly how do you feel?

Mylz gazed a crossed the table at Tonya he wanted her in his arms bad.

Tonya glanced over at Mylz and she explained that she felt confused about what was going on with her.

How did this happen? Was this there all the time and I didn't know it?

Tonya was full of questions.

Mylz walked over to where Tonya was sitting and said calm down we will get through this.

I'm really not sure I never seen this in any of your other x-rays.

Tonya drew in a long breath and looked up into the sky.

Mylz felt bad because he had no answer he wanted tonight to be different he needed to be the man who new what to say and do but nothing came to mind.

He really wish things could be different at this moment.

Well Tonya said, it is what it is, I really wanted to talk to you about something else any way.

Switching, the subject.

Mylz looked surprised.

Tonya stared out in to the city until she could gather all her thoughts and look Mylz in the eye.

Tonya forced a smile as she turned around, So tell me Dr the truth will I be to forward if I told you that I'm very interested in you on a personal level.

I consider my self lucky he said in an incredibly soft voice.

Oh, and why is that?

I think to be honest you are the most beautiful woman that I know.

Tonya was taken back she never assumed that he felt like that.

She know that he maybe liked her but not like that.

I've been wanting to talk to you about this for a while and never wanted to cross the Dr. Patient lines.

Who set those lines? Tonya asked smiling.

Tonya got up and walked pass Mylz taking his glass out of his hand let me get you a fresh drink.

Tonya felt her face getting red she tried to be bold and Mylz said more than she expected.

He was in love with her and she just didn't know what to say.

For someone who always played by the rules tonight Mylz was breaking everyone he knew.

I'm just going to put it all on the table and see what happen he thought to him self.

Aw man it's been a while I don't even know how she's going to take me especially at this time in her life.

Mylz seen Tonya coming out with drinks and meet her at the door. How are you feeling?

I'm good I'm just shocked by how you feel, I kind of thought you liked me but I'm the most beautiful woman you know yeah right.

I figured that you were involved with some one.

I fell for you a few months after you arrived in my emergency room.

Shut up Tonya said playfully.

I did Mylz said looking her in her eyes, you took my breath away I could not believe that some one could hurt you like that cat did.

I watched over you night and day while your were in the hospital.

Wow! Tonya said in amazement.

Is your drink to strong Tonya asked playfully?

Honestly Mylz I here what your saying, you know what I'm going through to me time is of the essence ok.

I'm attracted to you in a way that surprises me. But.

Before Tonya could say anything else Mylz was in her face, let's just take it one day at a time he said as he kissed her lips softly.

What a year this has been Tonya thought.

Tonya returned the kiss she placed her arms around

Mylz neck and heat began to rise in both of there body's.

Your going to make it girl, I'm going to make sure of that.

Look at me Mylz whispered I care about what happens to you.

As she looked in to his eyes she could feel an attachment to this man, impressed by his words she just wanted to stay in this moment, stay standing here with his arms around her this felt good.

Suddenly Tonya felt faint oh not now she thought not now.

Mylz caught her just as she passed out.

Carrying her limp body to the couch Mylz was concerned.

Just a few seconds later Tonya woke up.

Dmm what happen did I do it again?

This has got to stop Tonya said with a little anger in her voice.

Mylz just held her close to him Tonya needed that affection.

Mylz held here like he was about to loose her and she wasn't even his YET.

Tonya looked up at him his eyes were glazed like he wanted to cry, this made her sad

What's up she asked?

I just want you better he said in a soft voice.

He looked down into her eyes and kissed her I really want you to be all right.

Tonya took Mylz face in her hands and kiss him back it felt good I want you Tonya said I really want you.

Man I'm just glad to be here with you now Mylz said.

Thank you for dinner and the invite it's been a while since I've spent time with a beautiful woman in my arms.

Ring ring

Who is this Tonya thought to her self?

Excuse me Tonya said as she reached for the phone on the coffee table.

Damm it's Milo what could he possible want at this time of night.

Hey man what's up.

Hey sis how's it going?

All is well Tonya said softly, why.

Well I just got to the house and mom told me to call you and check on you and see if you are all right.

Yeah I'm fine I'm here chilling thats it.

Oh, that cools how was your day?

Milo asked because Tonya was talking like she had a little rush in her voice.

Are you alone?

Why did you ask me that?

Because it sound like you're in a hurry to get off the phone is something going on? Is any one there?

Before she scared him to death she had better tell him, every one has been so nervous for her to be alone since that man assaulted her.

Yes Milo Dr. Freeman is here with me.

What are you ok?

Yes baby I'm fine we are having a little cocktails and dinner if you don't mind.

OH I see cool that's all you had to say, Keep your clothes on Milo said.

Shut up Tonya said through her laugh I'll talk to you tomorrow by boy.

You and your family are very close I like that Mylz said.

By this time Mylz was getting tired and it was about to be 11:45pm and he had to be at work early in the morning.

Hey it's getting late and I must be leaving, he said as he looked at Tonya.

Tonya sat the phone back on the table.

Mylz stood up, adjusted his shirt, took Tonya hand, and helped her up.

I need to get going and get some rest.

Tonya looked uneasy.

Are you ok?

Yes I'm fine.

Mylz placed his arm around Tonya's waist tonight was great I would like to see you in the morning.

Oh yeah Tonya thought to her self I want to see you in the morning to right in my bed.

Tonya smiled.

What was that thought Mylz asked.

It was funny as much as he wanted Tonya he knows that tonight was not going to be the night.

Tonya had fainted and she appeared weak and a little tipsy, that could be a good thing he thought to him self.

Mylz took both hands and wiped his face as he shook his head.

Tonya anticipated making love to Mylz tonight after she passed out she know that he might not want to be physical with her but she was going to try anyway.

Hey you know that you've been drinking, why don't you stay her with me you can rest here for a while and leave later.

Tonya smiled inside.

Mylz Agreed with Tonya because he wanted to keep his eye on her tonight anyway.

Intrigued with Tonya invite Mylz sat back down.

Let's go in my room Tonya said as she grabbed Mylz hand.

Tonya has a beautiful bed room with a large retreat in it with a double sided fireplace and a 70 inch plasma on the wall it would be nice to kick it in there she planed.

Mylz follow in silence, watching Tonya walk in front of him. Eyebrows raised.

Entering Tonya's bed room he was impressed she's a woman with great since of style he liked that.

Hey I'm going to jump in the shower right quick turn on the TV if you want or just feel free to lie across the bed and rest.

Tonya was comfortable with Mylz in her house and in her room he had taken care of her and her body for a long time.

Don't take to long I'll miss you Mylz said playfully.

I want Tonya said back, join me she said as she turned around looking over to where Mylz was standing.

Shock he stood there. Yeah right he said.

Did you think I was playing when I told that I want you?

Tonya asked with a smirk on her face.

Mylz was not going to wait any longer to claim his girl he started walking towards Tonya.

She know that maybe she should not have said that she actually got a little nervous.

As she watched him getting closer to her the nervousness went away.

She stood there waiting Mylz started kissing her lips as he ran his fingers through her hair.

Tonya gave in to his touch.

What I thought would never happen was happening Mylz and I showering together looking a this package Pleased Tonya just smiled.

Mylz stood behind Tonya with his arms wrapped around her tiny waist you feel so good he said in her ear.

Tonya felt heat her body getting warm, was it the shower are this man that was in it with her?

Tonya turned and began rubbing the soapy washcloth all over Mylz body.

Mylz could not take it any more; I want you he said as he kissed her hard I need you he whispered.

The shower door open Mylz reached out and picked up a towel that was placed on the counter

And dried Tonya beautiful body and him after.

Mylz heart was beating nice and slow he picked Tonya up and carried her to the bed.

Slowly kissing her and placing her on the bed he began to just look her over, wow he said your beautiful.

Tonya reached up and took his hand and pulled him close to her kissing his neck, his chest, his lips

Tonya body became tense; I could smell him I could feel his man hood raise.

Slowly he lay his body on me my heart was beating fast like I was a school girl and this was my first time.

I know that it's been a while but damm. I hope I'm not breathing as loud as I think I am.

Slow down girl

Tonya told her self don't pass out again.

Mylz asked her are you all right softly as he reach for her breast and began to rub it.

Yes she said with a low voice that fells good moaning and moaning closing her eyes

Tonya relax stay focus don't faint she reminded her self.

Mylz kept up the exploring of her body this is what he has wanted for a long time so he was definitely going to make this last.

He felt his man hood get hard but he was not finish exploring her body with his lips and tongue.

Tonya moans louder as he started sucking my breast this was a very sensitive part of her body she really enjoyed when they got attention.

Slowly Mylz started working his way down her body,

Mylz heart started pounding he was kissing her stomach and he could smell the aroma of Tonya juices and it was making him tingle.

Mylz went lower he wanted to be closer to the spot his lips went lower Tonya could feel the heat of his breath she arch, her back her body was throbbing from the inside out.

Oh Damm. Mylz heard her say.

Slowly he started kissing her wetness she could fell his tongue licking up and down her spot oh, oh Tonya moaned as he sucked and made his tongue dance on her clit.

She stared rubbing Mylz bald head as he worked his magic.

Oh baby Tonya said, your making me so wet Mylz kept doing what he was doing.

After tonight he thought you will be mind.

Mylz raised up looking into Tonya beautiful face her eyes was close all he wanted to do tonight is to please her.

Damm, Dr, he heard her say. working his way back up Tonya's body. Tonya took control she was ready to make sure he was pleased as well.

Tonya rolled Mylz on his back climbing on top she began to suck and kiss on his chest while reaching and finding his man hood she caressed the length of his large stiff bar slowly she could feel him entering her, I sat up straight taking in every inch squeezing every muscle in her body.

I want to take the tip off that thang, moving up and down I could fell the large head I got so wet.

Her wetness played a tone that sound real good to Mylz ears.

Mylz stared at me as I moved riding him like a brand new Mustang.

He held my waist and tried to control my movement, but tonight I'm in control because there just might never be another one for me.

Damm Girl, Damm slow down baby slow down please don't make me I heard him beg.

My eyes stayed on him, smiling I wanted him to know just who he was dealing with.

I bend down and kissed his beautiful lips and than position my self in a squat I kept moving as his bar disappeared and reappeared over and over again.

Oh yeah I like that she thought, suddenly Mylz grab my waist held me down and began to shake out of control Damm, Damm he said as his breath got heavy.

Are you ok? I ask smiling.

O yeah.

That's not fair he said smiling.

He lay on his back holding me your awesome but we're not finish yet.

I eased off of him but he was not letting go where are you going?

Feeling real relaxed I lay back down.

Making love is like exercise to me the more I get the more I want.

Anxious to get started again I began to rub Mylz.

After about ten minutes Mylz was up and ready to make love again.

This time he lead and I followed he entered with a thrust he know he could last longer this time so he took his dick and worked it like magic in and out he moved making sure I felt every inch, it was perfect.

He set a pace and I matched move for move he pushed deeper and I accepted all he was offering, we went from position to position hitting it from the back, the side one leg on his shoulder and the other in the air we made love like we would never see each other again.

Ring Ring.

Tonya looked over at the clock on her night stand, it was nine thirty. Quickly raising up and wiping her hair out of her face, how did I sleep so long the thought rushed through her mind grabbing the phone Hello she said quickly?

Girl what happen to you this morning why are you still home and not at the gym.

Wow! She said as she felt the soreness of her back and body.

Tonya looked over and saw the Dr Freeman had all ready left and theirs a note on the pillow.

Oh shoot girl I over slept.

You have never over slept are you all right?

Yes I'm great just sore.

What happen did you hurt your self? Did you fall again?

Yeah I fell right in Mylz arms and on his.

What no no you did not, you and Mylz no you did not.

Yes I did that's why I missed the gym this morning and girl if you had not call I would still be sleep.

Where is he?

Hey I don't know he must have left to go home and change and get ready for work.

All I see is this note that say Thank you beautiful I'll call you later.

Screaming Christina said you better tell me everything like they did when they were in college.

Well I can tell you this he's an awesome lover that knows how to take his time pleasing.

He is defiantly packing, and not afraid to go down.

Girl he blew my mind I'm so sore we went for hours.

Girl shut up, I'm so happy for you I hope you did not pull your squat move on him.

Oh yes I did and it worked he could not hang I just smiled I still got it girl.

The funny part about it he grabbed me by my waist and shook so hard I thought he was having a heart attack he finally start slowing his breathing down and I know he was all right.

Christina was laughing hard her stomach was hurting.

Seriously Tonya said I do need to talk to you about something, where are you?

On my way home do you want me to stop by?

Yeah if you got time I'll put on some coffee, I needed to get up and shower I'll see you when you get here.

Christina got to the house and knocked on the door.

Tonya walked out of the kitchen with two cups of coffee; she set one on the hall table so she could open the door.

What's up girl Christina said as she walked in.

Here Tonya said as she reaches Christina her cup of coffee.

Let's go in the liven room and sit, I need to tell you some thing and don't get mad ok.

What the heck are you talking about?

Well this is what's going on with me before I go tell mom dad and Milo I just wanted your support.

I saw Dr Freeman yesterday and Damm he was awesome no not for real ok, any way let me clear my thoughts.

Wow! Tonya said fanning her self.

Cool it tramp tell me Christina said laughing.

All right Tonya said as she looked towards the ceiling.

He told me yesterday that I had to take all of these crazy test, and after that x-rays she said as she got up off the couch and walked over to the patio door.

Her voice started getting soft and here eyes began to water.

Tonya what's the matter you're scaring me Christina said as she walked over to her and placed her hand on her shoulder.

You're crying what's this about

Tonya stared out into the sky before she said another word.

Is something going on with your heart again? Christina asked softly.

No.

It's my head.

What? I don't understand.

He found a small spot on my brain and . . . .

What? What are you trying to tell me Christina yelled?

Tears were now forming in her eyes what the fuck is going on?

Christina hugged Tonya tight.

Please, please, don't Christina said crying?

Tonya started crying harder I just wanted you to know why I keep passing out she said through her tears.

What are we going to do Christina asked?

Wiping her tears Tonya said I have to tell Mom, dad and Milo before I make that decision.

Ill be going over there in a few and talk to them about it I was hoping that you would go with me.

Of course I will Christina said wiping her tears trying to be strong.

So what is Mylz wanting to do?

Well he wants' to go ahead and have me check in and have an emergency surgery that's what he said.

Oh my god Christina said.

I'm so afraid Tonya said as a new stream of tears ran down her face. Man a difference a day makes.

We were just on top of our game life was good I was a top Realtor showing and selling homes and now I can't even think.

I don't even know what day or date it is some times.

I don't know how to tell mom and dad this new drama I just want to ball up and die.

How can I keep hurting them?

You need not worry about that you need to tell them they would want to know.

We just have to get through this Christina said softly we can do this.

After a few cups of coffee and emptying out the tissue box the girls drove to The Gardeners house to meet with the family.

The honest to god truth was that Tonya did not want to tell them.

Knocking on the door and twisting the knob the door was unlocked, Damm mom still never lock her door Christina said smiling.

She thought back to when she was a child and lived down the street every time she came by she would just knock and walk in Tonya house the door was never locked.

She smiled and thought it felt good to be in this house.

Ring ring ring.

Mom where are you? Tonya yelled through the house as she walked towards the kitchen.

Hello Tonya said as she picked up the Phone.

Hello, is this Tonya?

Yes it is. Who is this?

I'M going to kill you B.i.t.c.h.

The phone dropped out of her hand just as Christina walked in.

What happen Christina asked?

Are you ok?

It's him it's that bastard that hurt me she said.

Looking around nervous thinking, he was watching her from the next room.

What? What did he say?

Where's my mother she said quickly.

Mom, Mom she yelled.

Grabbing the phone Christina yell who is this?

I'm going to kill you BITCH.

Christina got real mad.

If you fell froggy motherfucker leap I'll be waiting for your ass.

Tonya came back with a panic look on her face. Moms not home and her car is in the garage.

Call her cell Christina said as she covered the phone with her hand.

I'll fix you the voice said you're a tramp and you will die.

Christina motion for Tonya, come here.

He is still on the phone she whispered Tonya had talked to her mom she was out with the lady next door they had went to play bingo at the recreation center.

Tonya went into the hall to grab the other phone as she put the phone to her ear she heard the man on the line say I'm coming for you when you least expect it.

You know what Tonya said your bitch ass don't scare me you got the jump on me because I was not expecting that shit but bring it bitch I'll be where u need me to be.

Just than Milo walked in and heard his sister sounding like she was in high school and she was getting ready for a show down.

He had a flash back.

The girl at Tonya Jr. High school that wanted to fight her because her boyfriend kept watching Tonya.

Her name was Gina, Very cute but no confidents.

She some how got our house number and kept call the house and threaten Tonya.

Tonya was definitely not having that she had to be stopped and she was going to do that in a hurry.

Tonya model was when someone is looking for you flip the scrip you go looking for them.

Thing were just not sounding right in his sister voice he haden seen her mad in a long time.

What's up Milo asked looking at Tonya and than Christina.

Neither answered.

Bring it. He heard Tonya said loud, Christina yelled in the phone we will beat you down you just try steeping this way you got yours coming.

Tonya put her hand over the phone and Told Milo that it was the person that beat her in the vacant house.

Milo started steaming he took the phone from his sister and said who is this?

Suddenly the phone hangs up.

You scared him Christina said as she came into the hall, This Mofo is bold and how did he get this number.

They all went into the den and sat down Christina call Kenny and was filling him in on what just happen and how Tonya wanted to jump through the phone on this man.

Tonya and Milo was talking.

Milo said how dare he call this house I'll show this mofo better than I'll tell him.

We'll go looking for him instead of him come looking for us.

Milo began making phone calls.

Milo wanted to find this guy before the police so after Tonya got out of the Hospital Milo had his Mother and his sister phone taped.

He pulled out this device and looked at the caller Id and locator and saw that the call had came from a couple cities away.

Fifteen minutes later the door bell rang and twelve of Milo boys were at the door and on their way in.

What's up sis the guy's said to Tonya and Christina as they walk through the den and into the garage?

It's on now Tonya thought she and her family was not about to take a chance with this crazy person.

I think we should call the police Christina said as she thought about what was about to go down.

Detective Dent was really nice we just need to inform him of what just happen don't you think?

Hell to the NO, Tonya said out loud let's fuck his ass up first and than call the police.

She said as she shook her head and struck a pose like she was paparazzi ready.

Milo located the number that the call had come from and sent Matthew to the address just do a drive by because he lives in that city actually not far from the address. Ten minutes later Matthew calls and tells every body that the phone call came from a phone both that is in front of a laundry mat.

That mofo Milo said, this dude is up to his old tricks.

Why is this guy calling my mother's house she asked herself?

Tonya kept thinking how did he get this number I had just meet this guy that day.

I never put my mom's number on anything this was puzzling to her.

Tonya are you going to tell mom what's going now? Christina asked.

Tonya stood there thinking how she was going to tell her mom or if she was.

Let's go Tonya said as she grab Christina's arm.

Where are we going?

To my office I need to check on something.

Mylz was thinking of his night with Tonya as he took a break from his busy morning.

Wow he thought I need to call her he thought as he reached for his cell phone a page went across the intercom.

Dr. Freeman you're wanted in the E R.

I'll call later he said as he started over to the E R department.

A woman name Lisa who is very up set she tells me that her son can't feel his feet.

As I enter the room I see a young man lying on the bed and a tall gentleman standing by the bed.

Hi I'm Dr. Freeman tell me what's going on.

Hi I'm Mike and this is my son Mark he played football last night he is a senior at Gardenia High.

He played a great game last night and he seemed ok afterwards we just went home and went to bed that's it.

I don't understand Mike said with a feared looked on his face.

Lisa was pacing the floor what is wrong with him she kept saying her arm crossed over her chest.

Mark how are you son? Can you feel me touching you Mylz asked?

No.

I'll order some blood test; we have to wait for it to come back and than move forward.

Mylz walked out of the room and over to the nurses station to give the order for the blood test.

Yes Dr. the nurse at the station said as she walked away.

After about five minutes Lisa ran from the room please come in here the numbness has moved up his legs and now his thigh's are numb to.

Mark can you feel this I ask as I pinch his thigh really hard.

No Mark said as tears start to run down the corner of his eyes.

What is going on I thought as I pinch the back of Mark's leg without any reaction.

Excuse me I said as I walked out of the room.

I was thinking that this could be Guillain Barre Syndrome (GBS) but it doesn't move through the body that fast.

It was about forty five minutes later the blood work was back I was hoping my answer came with it.

As I was looking over the test I was shocked to see that Mark's Potassium level was the lowest I have ever seen.

I called the lab so that they could reconfirm the test result.

This is Dr. Freeman in emergency and you did a test on Mark Williams's right.

Yes Dr. How can I help you Keith asked?

Dr Freeman I ran that test three times to make sure the numbers were right.

Thank you Dr Freeman said. I walked into Mark's room and I asked his parents can you come out here please.

I had to move fast before we lose this kid, I told the parents that Mark had a very low potassium level and the medicine he need's is very dangerous it could help him or kill him if we don't move fast.

I told them that I had never seen any thing like this.

I got permission to move forward with the meds to save Mark's life.

I call in another Dr to assist we started to give the meds through Mark's Iv tube making sure not to give it to fast and not to move to slow because the numbness was moving up his body in a fast pace it had already reached his waist line.

After a few minutes, I asked Mark to move his toe and right in front of my face this kid was getting better.

It was a great feeling and it brought back to mind that great time he had last night with Tonya a big smile came across his face.

Thank you, Thank you Lisa repeated.

Tonya and Christina headed towards her office Christina looked over at Tonya tears were falling.

What's up?

Tonya was reflecting on her brutal assault, the call was the rocket that hit home that finally made her want to have her one last cry.

Tonya cried so hard that she had pull over and park, Christina held her friend tight.

Its ok she said this is just a little set back girl.

You know what they say a set back is just a set up for a come back.

Your back you could have died I'm grateful that you're still here.

Silent tears welled up in Tonya eyes as she pulled back into traffic she reached up and wiped her tears.

After getting to the office Tonya went over to her desk, looking around she could fine nothing with her personal information on it.

She sat in her chair to clear her thoughts.

Shaking her head Christina asked what are you looking for?

I meet this guy over the phone here right.

Now how did he get my mothers number?

We talked while I was here in the office and he set the appointment, we than meet a day later at the laundry mat.

I haven't fill out anything with my mother's information on it in years she said.

Tonya thought how?

Girl this is the only Job you have ever had and you were living at your mom's when you got this job.

Tonya sat at her desk and booted up her computer let's see something she said.

Tonya pulled up her personal file that the Real Estate Company has on her.

And their it was her name with all of her mother's information the address, and phone number on it.

This bastard has a way of getting into Realtors personal information.

We need to call Detective Dent Christina said with a little shake in her voice.

I think I will before another Realtor get hurt.

Now listen Christina said we need his help right now because that group Milo put together is not there for a party and we don't want none of them in prison.

Tonya cell phone rang.

The call ID said unknown.

Christina and Tonya looked at each other who is it Christina asked softly.

Tonya turned the phone her way so she could read the ID box.

Answer it girl you are a Realtor you know that you get calls from every where

He will not punk us like this that not an option oh hell naw.

Hello Tonya Gardener how can I help you?

Hey you she here Mylz sexy voice on the line.

A big smile came across her face; hey you back how are you she said very sexy and low.

The memories of last night took over her thoughts

I feel great what about you?

I want to cry but I can't.

What Mylz asked with concern?

My day started off just great after I over slept which I never do she said playfully.

Than I just got a threaten call from the bastard that hurt me.

What!

Mylz yelled in the phone as he walked into his office closed the door and sat at his desk.

Yeah he called my mother's house just by luck I answered the phone.

I went there to tell her about my situation but she wasn't home the phone rung so I answered it.

You're kidding right Mylz said.

No I think this guy has something to do with the Real Estate business.

Why do you say that?

It's been over Six Realtors assaulted in the last two years that we know of and they are all woman.

Four did not make it and two of us made it out alive.

Just than Tonya remember her call and wonder if the other woman had gotten a call as well.

Baby hold on she said quickly.

Christina I think your right we do need to call Detective Dent we need to know about the other woman.

Christina jumped from her chair, raced over to the desk, picked up the phone, and dialed the police department.

Detective Dent how may I help you.

Detective this is Christina from the hospital, you helped my friend Tonya Gardener.

Yes I remember you.

What going on?

Tonya received a call from the man that assaulted her.

What!

What time was this and where did she get the call?

It was at her parent's home and we just discovered that this guy must be some how associated with the Real Estate business because . . .

Wait Detective Dent said quickly slow down Christina.

Well the only way he could have gotten her mom's number is off her personal file.

This is the only job she has had since we have been out of College.

He called her about one hour ago can you do something?

What about the other woman the women that fought him off.

Detective Dent got quiet it had not been released yet, that another woman was found in one of the Foreclosed property on the west side.

Are you there she asked.

Yes I'm just writing down what you telling me.

Have you heard from the other woman yet?

No Christina but I'll call her to check on her right now

Where is Miss Gardener?

She's right here she's all right where at her office that's how we figured out where this guy got her information from.

Hey you to be good let me do all the detective work I'll call you all back in a few.

Thank you Christina said slowly I hope she's all right please call us when you find out.

Will do Detective Dent said talk to you soon.

Christina cell phone rang.

Hello.

Hey Christina have you heard that a Jane doe was just brought in to the emergency room and she was found on the west side in a property that had been up for auction.

A Realtor was setting up for the auction and found her in back bedroom.

What!!! Are you sure Kim?

Yes I'm sure; she is in grave condition, between me and you Christina I think it's that girl that was here before.

Christina got quiet.

Hey are you ready to go? Tonya said as she walked over to where Christina was standing.

What happen? Did you talk to Detective Dent?

Yes I did he's going to check on the other woman and call us later.

But girl guess what? I just spoke to Kim and she said that a woman was just brought into the emergency room and she was found in a home that was up for auction on the west side.

Mylz didn't mention that to me.

I think it just happen while you guy's was on the phone.

Lets go over and see what's up Tonya said do you think that they would let us see her.

After getting to the hospital Tonya and Christina stop by Dr. Freeman office to see if he knows anything about the woman that was brought in.

Where is he?

He's not in his office Christina said after she knocked and stuck her head in.

He must be in the emergency department let's go over there.

As they walked to the emergency department Mylz was coming down the hall.

Dr. Freeman how are you Christina said in her professional voice.

Hey you two what's up? Looking surprise.

Mylz looked over at Tonya are you all right he asked.

Yes were here to see the lady that was brought in, she was found in the vacant house that was up for auction on the west side.

Wow! Yes I know the one you're talking about, I just heard

Did you see her Tonya asked quickly?

Yes I did.

Well is she ok?

No sorry, shaking his head you're too late she passed about Ten minutes ago.

Tonya asked Mylz was she the Realtor that came here a few months ago.

You know I never seen that lady she was not in need of my services at that time.

I just happen to be in the emergency Department a minute ago and Dr. Wilson caught me passing by and asked for some assistant.

She is still down there but she was beat bad he said sympathetically.

We will see you in a minute Christina and Tonya said as they started walking down the hall in a rush to get a look or name of this woman.

Tonya could here a woman screaming and crying why, why Lord why.

As we got closer we could see who was yelling.

Christina knows that face it was the mother of the young lady that came in a few months ago.

She turned quickly and looked at Tonya, It is her that's her mother I meet her the first time she was here.

That fucken Bastard Tonya said.

Tonya took out her cell phone and dialed Milo phone.

What up sis.

Milo he did it that Bastard killed that other girl the one you told me about when I was in the hospital.

Where are you Tonya asked very frustrated?

What, What?

Where are you? And how do you know that?

I'm at the hospital right now, she was found in a house that Jack was doing an open house and auction in.

Are you still with Christina?

Yes she's right here.

I'm still at the house the boys are out, this dude is marked so lay low, and I'll call you in a few.

Thanks I want his ass caught; this is bull shit she said angrily.

Christina was talking with the mother and trying to find out just what happen.

All of a sudden Tonya anger got the best of her, she started feeling faint and down she went hitting the floor hard.

Christina went running to her side I need a Dr. She yelled.

Please some one help me.

All the nurses ran toward them from the nurse station that was a few feet away.

Laura, was at the nurse station got on the intercom and call for Dr Wilson.

Dr. Wilson please come to the Emergency Department with fear in her voice.

Mylz and Dr. Wilson were standing in the hall not to far talking when the call went out.

Come on man let's go see what's up I may need your help again Dr. Wilson said humorously.

As they turn the corner Mylz could see Christina on the floor over Tonya and he took off running.

What happen?

She passed out Christina yelled, help her panic all in her voice.

Move Mylz said.

Mylz bent down and listen to see if she was breathing Tonya he said.

Mylz and Dr. Wilson picked her up and took her into an empty room.

She fell so hard Christina said through her tears please help her.

We need to get a CT scan stat Mylz yelled at the nurse that had started an IV on Tonya.

Yes Dr.

Tonya looked so helpless.

Hang in there girl Christina said as she kiss Tonya on the cheek I'm here.

After a few seconds Tonya was being taken in to the trauma center of the hospital and in to the room for her CT scan.

Dr. Freeman right by her side.

Dr Wilson monitored the scan as the pictures started coming through he saw that Tonya was in need of emergency surgery.

Dr. Freeman, can you come in here? Dr. Wilson asked.

Man, you know what need to be done you see this right?

Mylz wiped his face I know man we need to do this now.

Christina walked in with Tonya's Mother she know what was up and it was time to do something.

Tonya was unable to give permission for the operation so her mother signed all the paper work.

Christina had called the house to speak to Milo and Mr. gardener answer the phone.

Through her tears she was able to tell him what was going on.

Milo was still there and brought him to the hospital.

On the way he and his father said nothing.

After about an hour and a half Mylz came out and let the family know it was a close call but all is well and Tonya is going to be all right.

Mrs. Gardener got up and gave him a big hug can I see her now?

Well she is in recovery she will be out for another hour or so but yes you can see her.

Mr. Gardener and Milo shook Dr. Freeman hand as they passed him headed towards the recovery room.

Christina was already in the room, when the family came in they all hugged as the surrounded

The bed.

Baby Mrs. Gardener said I'm here why didn't you tell us she said in a low tone.

Mr. Gardener felt tears well up in his eyes this was not happening again he bent down and kissed her face I love you he said.

Milo stood there in disbelieve how could she be hurt again?

Milo felt like he was on the show punked and Ashton Cusher was going to jump out with his camera any minute.

Or was God just mad at his family, naw that's not it, but what is it.

Milo walked out of the room he could not stand to see what this person had his family going through.

Milo headed for the elevator, as he pulled out his cell phone.

Hurry up Milo said to as he stood there for what seemed like an extremely long time the elevator opened.

During the ride down to the first floor a couple of nurses chatted about the woman that was found in the house on the west side.

Milo heard one of them say that she was beaten so bad that her left side of her face was caved in.

Milo felt like steam was coming out of his head he just wanted out of this elevator.

The doors open and he rushed out immediately needing to get out into the air.

Milo recalled just how much he didn't like the hospital.

Just for that brief moment, he thought he was going to fly off the handle.

Hey man Milo said after dialing James number, where are you?

Yeah man she out of the operating room she's in recovery thanks for asking.

Where's the rest of the crew?

James started telling him where everyone were.

I want every one at my house in Fifteen minutes make the calls and I will see you there Milo said and hung up the phone.

Kenny just arrived at the hospital as Milo was leaving the front door of the hospital on the way to his car.

What's up man? Kenny said how's Tonya?

She's in recovery on the Third floor every one's up there with her I'll be right back he said as he wiped the tears from his eyes and headed for his car.

Hey sweetie Christina said as Kenny walked into the room.

Kenny and Christina hugged.

Hello Mr. and Mrs. Gardener as he shook Mr. Gardener hand and hugged Mrs. Gardener.

Baby how is she doing? Kenny asked Christina.

She is just resting Dr. Freeman was able to help her, baby I was so scared she passed out and hit the floor so hard.

Wow! Kenny said as he held Christina and looking over at Tonya.

I'm really glad your here. Did you get a chance to get you something to eat?

Kenny just got off work.

No I came right from work, what about you, did you eat?

No, but I'm not very hungry.

I'm just thinking about Tonya's health right now.

Milo and the guy's are planning a mad hunt for this man and they are mad as hell.

Tonya woke up from surgery three hours later feeling tired and broke down.

Mylz was seated in a chair on the right side of her bed. Her Mother and father were on the left side stand looking over her.

Mom Tonya said in a very low voice what happen?

O thank you Jesus, baby I'm right here, her mom said as she kiss the side of her face.

They told me that you passed out in the hallway a while age.

Mylz woke when he heard the talking wow did I fall asleep?

Yes Dr you took a little cat nap Mrs. Gardener said.

How are you feeling Dr. Freeman asked?

It feels like a truck must have run me down.

No you just need to slow down.

It's all good now you should make a full recovery. I'm glad your awake.

I'm going to see you all later said Dr. Freeman as he headed towards the door.

Thank you, Mr. Gardner said as he extended his hand I know it's late but we thank you so much for your help.

Tonya laid back and closed her eyes she was in a little pain and she just wanted this day over and to wake up from this nightmare.

As the weeks passed, Tonya got better and was released from the hospital.

The hunt went on for the man that was committing the crime against Realtors.

Detective Dent has a drag net all across LA County.

Things were really getting bad in the LA county area the housing market is on a decline and Realtors are doing all kinds of advertising to get business they are using News Paper, Bill Boards, Inter Net Myspace, Face Book, Twitter and passing business cards out at every place they go.

The TV News are reporting that the economy is still heading for more problems in the weeks and months to come.

Today three woman were found murdered in three separate county's and the report said that they are waiting to get the identification on them before their names be released.

Detective Dent called a big meeting with the task force that he has created to find and arrest this guy.

Ok he said as the men took their seats around the round table. This guy has struck again and now it's three unidentified young Realtors that have been killed in the last few days. This guy is playing me and us for a fool and I don't like it one bit he yelled as he slammed his fist on the table on the board behind him was all of the young woman that he has killed over the past few months his portfolio was getting quite large.

This case needs to come to an end, I need every man in this room on high alert, looking high and low using all of your sources to find him.

Kenny went in to the office early this morning, he had a few thing that need to be close out on a case he had just finished and thing were about to slow down for him he thought, now I just might pop the question to Christina he said as he smiled to himself.

As he placed the last file in the cabinet he heard his secretary say hello sir how can I help you?

A deep voice said hello I'm look to retain a lawyer.

Ok, and what exactly will you be needing a lawyer for she questioned.

Kenny stepped out of his office.

Kenny look at the man standing in his reception area a well dressed brother tall built like pro ball player.

What can be this cats problem he thought to himself, lets see Kenny said to himself as he walked closer to this guy to shake his hand.

Shelia I'll speak with him Kenny said as they shook hands and Kenny lead him to his office.

What's your name Kenny asked as he handed his business card to the man.

I'm Charlie Washington.

Ok Mr. Washington how can I be of assistant to you.

Come on Miss thang get in this house your hair looks just fine.

I can't believe that witch cut my hair like this all I told her was to trim the ends Tonya yelled.

Girl please it looks great Richard said as he walked into Tonya front door, you are tripping

I need to talk Richard said with excitement, I was on the web the other night looking for me some fresh meat and girl I think I hit the jackpot he said as he put his hand over his mouth with his eye brows raised.

It was some freaky as shit going on, on this one sight Miss thang.

Wait before you start I need a cocktail Bitch because I know by your look you are going to be awhile

Tonya walked over to the bar to get herself a drink, what do you want Rich?

Pour me some white wine from the frig.

I need something cold I'm about to get hot girl.

Tonya laughs aloud.

Here she said as she handed him his white wine and took a seat next to him on the couch.

Well girl Richard started I went on this sight call DL Brothers dot hot one of my other friends told me about it.

It for brothers that's down low looking to hook up and make sexual connections.

That's some foul shit Richard Tonya said frowning her face you're kidding right.

It's a web site that cater to down low brothers.

Hell yeah and the menu is delightful Richard replied smiling.

Girl!

Black professionals who are single and some that are married.

Any way I meet this guy and we have been chatting for about six weeks.

Do you even know what he looks like Tonya asked?

Is he married? Does he have aids? Is he white are black?

Dang Miss thang let me tell you.

No is not married.

No he don't have HIV, and he is black.

How do you know?

Tonya and all of the girls were so protective of Richard he has never picked any one that the girls have approved of.

What ever, any way he and I are thinking about meeting next week.

We are going to meet in Long Beach down by the Queen Mary and take the tour.

Well that might be ok that's a public place.

I think he is the one Richard said.

How is he the one if you never saw him?

I haven't seen him because I was always at the hospital day and night with your ass.

Well I think your right I could not get you to leave you're the best Tonya said as she hugged him.

After Christina called me and told me what happen, girl I was not leaving you alone.

My mom and dad, Christina, Milo, and Kenny kept a around the clock watch on me.

Richard, tell me about your friend.

Ok he is 6ft 2 black weigh about 215 bald head, well dressed brother from what he tells me he likes most of the designers I wear, and he is a business owner.

Wait do he have a picture on his sight?

No remember he's down low Miss thang a lot of them don't post pictures.

Any way it's a skill to this just by the conversation you can tell if you really want to meet this person are not.

Wow! Tonya said.

Well what did you talk about for six weeks?

We talked about a lot of stuff like clothes, sports, other relationships and what we are looking for in a mate.

Girl we both are busy people me with my business and he with his also and the long hours I spent watching over you remember Richard said as he puff out his lips.

Well how are you going to know him when you all meet next week?

Down low brother have signals you may never see them do anything but another down low brother knows the signal all they do is make eye contact and a head raise.

A straight man, never look twice at a brother, but the down low brother would.

It is what it is girl.

Samuel is his name and he said that he will be letting me know what he will be wearing.

Tonya took another drink of her Patron and she was feeling real good.

Samuel is only able to get away he said from 6pm Friday and Saturday, and that works for me as well.

I love that web site I feel like a kid in the candy store.

Your so crazy Tonya said smiling.

I meet quit a few men who just want to hook up for a sexual fix and not get caught up but that's not what I'm looking for'

Yeah right Tonya said you know that you need a fix.

Well that's why I keep a few tricks in the background that I can call, I have pros in every area code Richard said as he covered his mouth.

I also found a Rapper, NFL player, and a NBA player; men who would travel anywhere to get a sexual hook up.

How do they advertise? Tonya asks with excitement.

Attractive professional black man, seeking other Attractive professional black males on the low.

Well sir Charlie said after he and Kenny shook hands and entered his office.

I'm looking to retain a lawyer for a friend of mind who has gotten himself in a little bind.

Ok, Kenny said I'm a criminal Lawyer is this a criminal case?

Yes but he don't know I'm here.

Well is your friend in jail, has he been arrested.

No.

I don't understand Kenny said.

What has he done that you think that he'll need a lawyer?

I'm just here trying to retain a lawyer just in case I here this is the best firm in the LA area.

Yes your right, I tell you what you have my card leave your card with my secutary and if you need this firm to represent your friend give me a call and I'll see what I can do.

Kenny extended his hand they shook and Charlie left after leaven his business card with Shelia.

Today was a nice day; Tonya decided to go to the Real Estate office

Good morning, Linda Tonya said to the office manager as she came through the front door and passed the big granted counter that Linda sits behind.

Hi Tonya!

Hey Tonya can you take this incoming call?

This lady is looking for an Agent to show her some homes.

Are you here to work; not knowing but very glad to see Tonya in the office.

Send the call over to my desk ill see what's up.

Oh and yes, I'm back.

I'm glad Linda said smiling

Good morning, Tonya said how could I help.

Good morning my name is Mona Dalton I saw a couple of homes in the La Bra area this weekend that are for sale and I would like to know if there still available and how soon can I get into them.

Ok sounds good.

Miss Dalton my name is Tonya and ill be glad to help you, but I need to ask you a few questions first.

Sure, Mona said.

Are you going to be the only buyer?

Yes.

Have you been pre qualified already by a lender?

Yes. I was pre qualified for 575.000.

Great Tonya said.

Do you have the address to the properties?

Yes.

Mona went on to give Tonya all of the address.

Ill look these up and Ill call you right back

Thanks Mona said with excitement my number is (310) 333-0978.

Ok give me a minute and ill let you know what I come up with.

Tonya and Mona made an appointment for 12:30 meet me at the office, Tonya said.

Ok ill be there Mona said very excited.

Mona arrived at the office at 11:45 Tonya was page to the front by Linda.

Hello Mona nice to meet you Tonya said as she extended her hand to Mona.

Like wise, Mona said.

Follow me I have all everything ready on my desk let me get them and we can be on our way.

Sounds great Mona said

I'm excited to finally have some one working with me.

The first property is a beautiful home that has three bedrooms and two bathrooms 2500 sq ft of living space in good condition.

Take notes Tonya advised Mona that is why I asked you to bring along a notebook you'll see every home will have things you like and things that you don't like.

Mona and Tonya headed to the second house, the home that I choose will be for my daughter she is hanging out with a bad crowed of young men and they got her on that stuff.

She is twenty three and has a little girl that I have custody of

I hope if I mover her away from the hood and over in a nice area that she might come to her reality.

Wow, I think that nice she is blessed to have a mother like you.

Oh yeah Mona said.

I would like to move fast this will be an all cash offer.

Ok were here Tonya said.

Smiling thinking to herself cash offer this is good this should be easy.

Tonya parks in the driveway gets out and get the paper with all the home information and combo to the lock box 5689 Tonya Said to herself as she walks over to the box to get the keys.

Tonya and Mona walk in to the house.

Nice Mona said with a smile on her face, large living room, nice hardwood floors, fireplace and lots of windows.

Let me open the blinds Tonya said as she walked over to the window.

This home is 3500 sq ft four bed rooms and three bathrooms it been on the market 35days.

That is good Mona said, I like it lets see the rest of the house.

Tonya headed to the bedroom while Mona headed towards the kitchen.

Standing in the kitchen Mona was very happy at the great condition of this home.

Tonya looks at the first bedroom it's a nice size.

The laundry room was next to this room the other two rooms were smaller by a few feet.

The master bedroom was at the end of the hall.

This was her first time showing homes sense the incident.

She looks down the hall at the back bedroom shaking her head.

Just than Mona comes out of the kitchen, how are the rooms she asked?

Nice so far Tonya said smiling, get it together girl she told her self.

All Tonya remembers is the long hallway leading to the back room.

Wow! This is a large room she heard Mona say loudly.

Tonya walked closer to the master bedroom at the end of the hallway, just as she entered the room Tonya screams and screams.

Mona comes out of the front bedroom quick to see what is going on.

We have to leave Tonya said, as she walked fast towards the front.

What is it, what did you see Mona asked with a shaky voice.

Tonya was shaking as she dialed 911.

Let's get out of here.

Mona was nervous she went and sat in Tonya's car, she could here Tonya tell the person on the phone that there is a dead woman in a vacant house 23678 Westlake Ave and that she is a Realtor showing the home and she stumbled up on this body.

Oh, my god Mona said.

I think she is a Realtor Tonya said on the phone she has a Realtor jacket on she told the person.

Oh, my god Mona kept saying as she listens to Tonya.

A car is no the way the operator said just stay out side.

Do not go back in a car is in route.

Are you all right Mona asked as she placed her arm around Tonya?

I'm ok ill call the office, have someone come, and get you.

Ok but will you be ok?

Yes, I'm ok.

A police car pulled up two police officers gets out in a hurry a second and than a third car pull up.

Tonya had called the office to have Mona picked up and John was on his way.

Tonya explained to the officer just what happen they took her statement as Christina pulled up in her car with Kenny in the passanger seat.

Kenny just arrived at Christina office when Tonya called.

You have to be kidding me girl what is going on.

Kenny came up and gave Tonya a big hug she was still shaking.

Lets get her out of here Kenny said.

I'll drive your car Kenny said you ride with Christina.

Tonya handed Kenny her keys, walked over to Christina car, and sat down, placing both hands over her face.

How in the hell did you happen to be the one who happen up on this shit? Was the door locked? Was there a smell in the house?

This is crazy what made you go to the office today.

The door was locked, there was no smell, and I was bored at home, any other questions Tonya said softly.

I am just so scared for you Christina said.

I'll be ok I need a stiff drink right now that's all get me home please.

Have you called Mylz yet? Did he know that you were going back to work today?

No and No.

Kenny was following the girls to Tonya house just as his phone rang.

Hello.

Hey, man Mylz said on the other line.

Hey man, Kenny said back are you on your way.

On my way where Mylz asked?

You haven't heard.

What Mylz said, I was calling to see if the four of us was getting together tonight.

Man I was in Christina office when Tonya called all messed up.

What! Mylz said confused.

Man she was showing a house today and found a dead woman in one of the rooms just about an hour ago.

What? Mylz said he was really tripping now

We are on are way now to her house call her man Christina and I just picked her up?

All Kenny heard next was a dial tone.

Mylz had left the hospital early today he had no idea what was going on.

Christina had got the call from Tonya about an hour ago while at work, she than told her assistant to call Dr. Freeman.

Kim tried to reach Dr. Freeman by phone she called his office and had him paged over the hospital intercom system but he never returned the call.

Christina phone started to ring the caller ID showed Kim's name yes Kim, What's up?

Christina Dr. Freeman never call back have you heard from him yet.

No but its ok I'll handle it, Thanks.

Tonya phone rang just as Christina finished her call.

Ring!

It Mylz Tonya said still shaking.

Answer it. Christina said

Hello. Baby, are you all right?

Yes I'm ok just a little shaken Tonya said in a soft voice.

I heard what happen I just spoke to Kenny; I am on my way ill meet you all at your house.

Ok. Tonya replied.

By six it was all over the evening news what had happen the body of a Realtor was found murdered no name was released.

Tonya was home surrounded by friends and family and detective Dent.

I hope that a press conference will bring attention to this killer detective Dent said.

What can the police do when a crime is committed and no one comes forward, Tonya asked angrily?

I'm hoping that is not the case this time.

After detective Dent left Things began to relax, I need another drink Tonya said.

Mylz walked over to the bar and fixed, Tonya a drink and brought it to her.

How are you? Kenny asked Christina.

This is just crazy I hope this guy will be caught soon.

This bastard is still up to his games and why was I the one that happen to find the woman Tonya yelled she paced back and fourth.

Ring! Ring.

Tonya raised one eyebrow who could that be she thought to her self.

She looked down at her ringing cellphone and saw that it was her mom phone number, looking over at her brother she asked did you tell mom?

Milo looked and shook his head no.

Ok that's good.

Hello, Mom.

Hi, baby did you here the news?

Yes Mom I did.

Christina shook her head do not tell her yet she whispered.

Everyone one knows how much she worries.

Are you ok, she asked tenderly?

Yes. mom I just fine a matter of fact I have a house full of company let me call you back ok.

Ok Ill talk to you later sweetie.

Richard showed up a few minutes after Tonya hung up the phone and sat on the couch.

Richard came to see if Tonya had heard the news but he could tell by all the company she had heard.

What's going on he asked.

The news said,

Christina stopped him before he could say another word.

Tonya found the woman.

What Richard said putting both hand over his lips, your kidding.

Oh, my I need a drink he said perplexed.

Everyone sat, talked, and just kept Tonya Company this was not a time for her to be alone.

Richard Phone rang and he saw that it was his new guy so he stepped out of the room to answer.

Mylz sat closer to Tonya I'm going to get something for you to eat and ill be right back, ok.

Hey I'll go with you man Kenny said.

Richard came back in with this big smile on his face.

What's up Christina and Tonya said at the same time.

Tell us some thing to break the mood Tonya said.

Are you sure Richard asked?

Yes, I'm ok.

Who is this new dude?

Girl Richard said with both eyebrows raised, my new friend wants to see me later.

I just might go he said poking out both lips it's been awhile if you know what I mean.

Bitch Christina said you're too many things.

What should I wear?

How serious are you with this new guy? Tonya asked.

I'm not.

Wear your Italian jean with that nice black button down shirt and the nice black boots.

O yeah! That will work he said smiling.

The men returned with the food. after eating and talking they all watched a movie.

Its getting late Christina said I'm going home ill check on you tomorrow.

Thanks ill call you in the morning Tonya said.

After everyone, left Tonya decided to go and take a bath and go to bed.

Richard meet up with his new friend at the Kodak Theater at one of their party area on the third floor.

Samuel was already there waiting for Richard, He and Richard had spoke earlier they know exactly what each other would be wearing.

Samuel ordered a shot of Patron and turned to look at the door to see if he saw Richard.

Richard had just arrive and was paying at the window of the club, and then started heading for the bar area.

Samuel stood up and waved him over mum Richard said as he headed towards the tall hunk of chocolate that was waving his way.

Nice shirt, nice shoes, nice jeans, and very nice smile Richard said to him self as he took a mental note, as he got closer.

Cha ching Richard said to him self.

Hello Richard said happily

Hello Samuel said very pleased to see such a nice looking man; well put together he thought to him self.

I order you a drink Samuel said as he turn to the bar and picked up the shot of Patron and handed it to Richard.

You did say you drink Patron.

Yes, that's what I said Richard said in his flirty voice.

So let's sit Richard suggested.

Sounds good Samuel said I have a booth over there for us.

Richard winked and he followed Samuel to the booth.

How was your day?

It's been one of those days.

Sipping my drink and admiring Samuel.

Looking at the people in the club having such a good time made me sink down in my seat and get relaxed.

Well it's been a slow day I just really relaxed today and kind of waited for this evening to come so I could finally meet up with you.

O Yeah, Richard smiled.

Well my day was crazy I need this drink.

Sipping his drink.

Wow like that.

Yeah.

One of my close friends had some trouble today that's all.

Man I hope she's ok Samuel said, with concern.

Richard and Samuel drinked, laugh and talked for a few hours and than went walking down then blvd enjoying each other's company.

Hello Tonya said.

Hey, sweetheart are you resting.

No not yet I'm just setting on the bed finishing some paper work.

Well Mylz asked do you need me to stop back by and help you get to sleep.

What Tonya said playfully?

Hell yeah she said to her self.

You heard me right Mylz said let me come and put you to sleep.

Put me to sleep Tonya laugh.

I think you was the one that fell a sleep first last time.

Laughing Tonya took the phone from her ear.

Mylz rubbed him self so is that a yes.

Laughing Mylz said you know that I had just worked a 33-hour shift at the hospital.

Say what you want Tonya laugh, the truth is that you can't handle this.

You had two options only handle it or get handled and you my dear got handled Tonya laughed.

Baby come over if you want I'll love to have you here even though you'll blame it on the long hours at work when you fall the sleep first.

Christina and Kenny stood in the kitchen and reflected on the wild and crazy things that happen today.

Babe I sure hope that this guy get caught soon

I wonder why Tonya took her ass to work.

Sweetheart Kenny said she has been off for a good while it was time

She wanted to get her life back on track.

But babe out of all the days

Detective Dent has this covered sweetie.

Well I guess so your right Christina said as she hugged him tight.

All right Kenny smiled don't start nothing you can't finish, Kenny said raising his eyebrows.

Oh, I can. what about you?

Let's go see she said as she led Kenny to the room.

Now what? Kenny said as he started kissing, rubbing, on her body slowly.

Christina slowly loosen Kenny belt and took his shirt out of his pants while kissing his full lips, moan and groans came from Christina.

Kenny knew what was going on with Christina she was on fire and he was ready to help extinguish her fire.

He reaches down pull's her blouse over her head and it falls to the floor.

Revealing her beautiful full breast

Damm Kenny said.

Tonya heard a small tapping on the front door and her stomach tighten she was surprise it was to soon for Mylz to be at the door.

Oh my it is Mylz she could see him through the glass window in the front door. Hey, Tonya said as she open the door.

Mylz walks right in, grab his girl, and start kissing her, and she kissed him right back.

Picking Tonya up off her feet I need you he whisper between kisses

I need you to.

Mylz put Tonya on the bed and began working his way up her body.

Tonya only wearing a robe, Mylz had already had that on the floor.

He began at her knees working upwards not missing a spot all he could hear was pleasure coming from Tonya.

Her body screams with pleasure taking her mind off her bad day.

This is exactly what she need and so did Mylz.

Mylz worked his way up Tonya's body kissing, sucking, and licking enjoying her beauty.

Tonya's breathing became faster and she wanted to explode wait, wait she said.

Mylz looked up confused.

I want you she said.

Mylz moved up closer Tonya pulled him on top of her.

Oh, ok Mylz said as he entered how's that he asked.

O Yeah Tonya groaned,

Yes, that's it.

Tonya worked in rhythm as they kissed and enjoyed each other matching beat for beat move for move.

That feels so good Mylz said as he held on to his girl.

Damm Mylz said with his eyes fixed on Tonya.

Work it he said as he watch Tonya ride him as if she was in a rodeo and she was going for the gold.

Slow down she heard him say, babe slow down your going to make me . . . .

Make you what?

You said you can handle me remember she laughed.

I know babe but . . .

No buts sweetheart, handle me or get handled.

Tonya tightens up and began to move slow and than fast teasing Mylz, she always made everything a work out.

Damm, girl she heard him say as his legs stiffen he was ready to pop.

Holding Tonya's waist tight he began to release.

Samuel and Richard saw each other every Friday and Saturday for about a month.

Richard working so hard during the

Week left him no time to socialize, Friday and Saturday is his only free time.

Richards's model is to never let someone work harder than him at his own business.

So he worked harder and it was really paying off it was nothing he wanted for except some one to share all of his success with.

Home, cars and clothes he had plenty all was missing is a great relationship.

Samuel hinted at a desire to be closer Richard notice but it was some thing about him that made Richard standoffish he liked him and he was trying to make sure he wanted Samuel to be the one.

If I was the old me Richard thought to him self I would have had his fine ass by now.

Something was very interesting and very strange about Samuel that made Richard slow down.

Richard thought of a plan ill give a cocktail party and let my girls give me their take on Samuel.

Yes, Richard said ill have a few friends over for a little fun.

Am I getting serious Richard thought I haven't even seen the goods.

After a few week's Richard and Samuel continue to see each other while Tonya, Christina and Richard put the cocktail party together.

The party invites went out along with a host of e-mails to all of their friends the party was three week's away.

Richard began to open up his schedule he and Samuel began to see each more meeting for lunch in the afternoon during the week and meeting for dinner on the weekends.

Still he had not yet slept with him he was holding out until after the cocktail party he plan on making that night very special.

Kenny and Christina were lying in bed talking about Richard's party that was coming up.

Baby I am not going to be dancing with a bunch of boy girls.

Laughing Christina asked what is a boy girl.

You know men dressing like girls.

Babe Richard has more girl friends than you and I put together.

You just stick with me and we will dance together she said softly as she kissed his lips.

Your worried about nothing, all of his parties are real fun you'll enjoy your self wait and see.

If you say, so Kenny replied.

You will see Christina said smiling.

Come here girl Kenny said in his sexy voice pulling Christina close to his chest.

Hugging her securely, I love you he said softly.

I love you, how was your day.

Did that strange guy come back?

Not yet, That dude was a very peculiar.

I wonder why someone who is not in trouble want to retain a Lawyer particularly an expensive Lawyer like you just in case.

Do you think he is a black terrorist?

Laughing Kenny said no Miss Detective.

Kenny started kissing her and it was on. He whispered I sure hope not my love.

It was the night before the party Richard, Christina and Tonya had been out running around all day looking for their outfits for the party.

All the drinks and food has been order and paid for the house is ready but finding the right gear was becoming more than a notion.

You know girl I always get the party jitters Richard confessed

Yeah-right Tonya said your ass just want to stand out in the crowed.

That will not be a problem.

Bitch Tonya said smiling stop acting like a queen you know the crown do not fit.

Dude is not all that Christina said, plus you haven't even brought him to meet us are given him none of the goods.

Laughing Tonya and Christina gave each other high five.

Laughing Richard said it's the mystery whore.

Pulling; his hands up to his mouth, raising his eyebrows.

I bet he's packing all tall guys are.

Your tall Christina said smiling.

If I showed you bitches my dark bar each one of you pointing his finger at Christina and Tonya would for sure leave your man I promise.

Maybe and maybe not Tonya said you are very fine I do say so my self, laughing loudly.

Let's go you girls are dreadful.

With bags in hands, they headed for the car.

Rodeo Drive is the best place to shop you can never leave empty handed Tonya said to Richard, looking in her bag admiring her dress and shoes.

Girl turn that up.

Stephane Mill I never know Love like this before is playing on the radio as they drove home.

It was the day of the party Richard was doing all of the final touches that need to be done.

The day was going great.

Samuel called Richard to see if he needed anything for the party and to confirm the time.

I have every thing you just get here when you can.

Ok sounds good I'll see you later.

Silence was all he heard next.

Hello Christina said, hey sweetheart.

Hi baby I'm running a little late so go ahead and go to the party and I'll meet you there just text me Richard's address.

Baby are you sure I can wait.

It's going to be a while because I have to close out this case file.

Ok.

Baby see if you can ride with Tonya so we want have two cars their.

All right that will work I'll see you there.

Tonya was getting dressed the music was playing in the back ground

Montell Jordan This is how we do it.

Ring Ring!
Hello.
Hey girl Kenny is running late what time are you leaving.
I'm getting dressed right now and Mylz is on his way.

Ok stop by and pick me up.
Ok will do I'll call you when we leave the house.

Richard Party was in full swing by the time Mylz, Christina and Tonya arrived people everyone were dancing, talking and drinking.

We all join in the fun got some drinks and started socializing Richard spotted Christina at the bar and made his way over to say hi.

Man this party is off the hook I see you invited everyone.
Well just about.
So where is the new guy.
He's not here yet.
Where's Kenny?
He will be here soon last minute things to take care of at the office.

Mylz and Tonya were enjoying the DJ playing all the latest hits from 1980.

After a few minutes Kenny arrived at the party He and Christina was out on the dance floor enjoying the party.

Richard danced around the room shacking his stuff and mingled with his guess

It was now about 11pm and the party was hopping.

Samuel just arrived on the block he could here the music from the party, parking his car he felt excited to see Richard.

The Dj started slowing the music down and took a five minute break as he played Maxwell Your Pretty Ways, Kenny took Christina back out to the dance floor and Tonya made her way to the bar.

Samuel walked through the front and Richard saw him hey Richard yelled waving him over to where he was standing.

Hey the party is jumping just like you said it would.

Yes people are still arriving.

Yeah I know it was a couple looking for parking when I was walking up.

So do you want a drink, Richard asked.

I really would like to use the rest room first if you can show me where it is.

Sure, follow me.

This is a very nice place.

The down stairs bathroom was busy someone was using it.

Trying to impress Samuel Richard let him go to the upstairs bathroom.

Tonya was in the hallway talking to Candy a girl from the gym.

Girl Richard, always have the best parties.

Who is that he's with Candy said in a lustful way.

Just as Tonya turned around Samuel walked into the bathroom Tonya got a small gimps at the side of his face.

I don't know she said I didn't see him.

He was a looker Candy said.

I got a man Tonya said playfully matter a fact let me go find him talk to you later.

Tonya headed back out side just as the D.J pumped back up the music and yelled over the mike every back to the dance floor to time to parrrrrrrrrtay.

Mylz pulled Tonya back on the dance floor and it was on.

Go Christina Go Christina.

Break it down Tonya yelled.

Tonya turned around to back that thang up and drop it like it's hot and spotted Samuel walking through the house.

What the fuck Mylz heard Tonya say.

What?

It's him she said as she turned to Mylz grabbing his arm and walking towards the house.

Mylz I saw him she said in a scared voice.

Him who?

Tonya shook her head knowing that she had been drinking, but she was sure she saw who she saw.

Baby What is the matter Mylz asked who did you see.

The guy, It's him Im sure all of a sudden boldness was all over her and she was ready to battle.

Out of the corner of his eyes Milo saw that Tonya looked like she had gotten very angry and he needed to find out just what was the problem.

Nothing was about to go down while he was around.

Richard was at the bar waiting for Samuel to come back so he could give him his drink.

There you are Samuel said.

Here you are handing him his shot of Patron.

Yeah this is great Samuel said in a very sexy voice.

Lets walk Richard said I have a lot of friends I want you to meet.

Lets do it.

Samuel and Richard bounced to the music as they headed for the patio.

Tonya and Mylz walked through the other side of the patio that led to the living room. Richard and Samuel walked through the door that led out through the kitchen.

It is so many people here Samuel said wow did you invite all of LA.

Where did he go she said, making her way through the people that are in the front area.

Milo came in after her what's up sis.

I seen that motherfucker he is here and I want him she said

Milo looked at Mylz and he look at him with raised eyebrows.

Milo shrugged who is here.

Walking fast through the crowed slow down Milo said tell me who did you see.

Tonya stopped in the kitchen turned around and scanned the crowed in the front room one more time.

Milo caught up to Tonya, who is here he asked again

The man that tried to kill me she said in a mad voice.

Where Milo said his anger level shot up one hundred per cent.

Mylz, grabbing her are you sure, what do he have on?

I'm sure I just saw his face.

Tonya spotted Christina and called her name.

Christina and Kenny turned around.

Tonya was waving her over.

She looks up set Christina said oh my I hope she's not drunk I'm just starting to have fun.

Girl he is here and I saw him he did not see me but I know what I saw.

What the hell are you talking about who?

That bastard that tried to kill me.

All right Christina said trying to calm her.

Milo, Kenny, and Mylz stood there no one know what this dude looks like but Tonya.

Richard and Samuel walked all around the patio and talked to people.

Richard introduced him to all of his friends and guess while they stood around and enjoyed the music.

Where are Christina and Tonya he thought to him self, they were on the dance floor he thought.

All of a sudden the music got louder Hey they heard the DJ yell get on the dance floor

Every body its time to do the electric slide.

People started for the dance floor in a hurry to get their spot.

It was so many people at this party that it was hard to see the face of the man that scared Tonya.

Well let's go out side Milo said he has to be here somewhere if that was him.

Milo, Kenny, Mylz got together lets separate and look for this dude Kenny said.

Tonya said I saw him you guys I know that I saw him and I'm not drunk.

Just as Tonya and Mylz went out the slid door through the liven room Kenny and Christina headed for the slide door near the kitchen Milo went towards the front door just to look and see if any one was out in front of the house.

Why are you two in here Richard said as he came through the slide door through the kitchen with Samuel following him.

Hey Christina this is my friend Samuel, Christina shook his hand, nice to meet you she said as

She winked at Richard.

Kenny back was turned to Richard and Samuel he was keeping his eye on Tonya.

Kenny Richard said, this is my friend

Kenny turned around to see the guy that stood in his office a week ago looking for a lawyer

For his friend that was not yet in trouble.

Hey man Kenny said as he reached to shake hands, good to see you again it's a small world he said.

Richard Look shocked how did they know each other, was Kenny a down low brother and he was keeping it from Christina,

Richard stood there with raised eyebrows.

Where is Tonya Richard asked?

She just went back out to the patio.

I want her to meet Samuel.

Ill go find her and than we will find you, Christina said as she headed out the door after Kenny.

Kenny pulled Christina by her arm just as she stepped out of the door, baby how do

Richard Know That guy.

Why?

That's the guy from the office that I told you about the one who showed up looking for a lawyer.

What? Your for real she said.

Yes. That's the dude I'm sure.

That's Richard's internet guy.

He met him off some web sight for down low brothers.

He's crazy than Christina thought to.

Tonya and Mylz walked around looking for the person that Tonya had seen.

Milo walked back through the front and Richard and Samuel was in the kitchen

Hi there Richard said did you leave and come back?

No. Why did you ask?

You just came through the front door I know you don't smoke and your date is all ready here looking for you.

Oh no man I was just looking for some one else.

Oh. Hey meet my friend Samuel

Milo reached out his hand and shook hands with Samuel I'm Milo He said.

Nice to meet you Samuel said.

Hey fellas I need a drink Milo said I'll see you all later.

Richard and Samuel took a break from the party for a little while to spend some one on one time together,

Where the hell, did he go Tonya said as she walked back in to the house.

Baby lets enjoy the party or we can call it a night let me get you a drink so you can calm down a little.

Ok. Your right let's have a good time I really want to enjoy Richard's party.

But if I see that guy again I'm going yell really loud.

The party goes on for another hour before Richard and Samuel comes back and joins the crowed.

Tonya and Mylz are on the dance floor having a great time when she see's Richard come

To the slide door and wave her way.

Tonya waves back just as she spots's Samuel.

Tonya eyes get very wide the words get caught in the back of her throat.

Tonya grab Mylz and spends him around and points at Samuel just as he spots her.

Samuel turns to make his way to the front door.

Wait Richard said what's wrong?

I have to get something out of the car Ill be right back.

Mylz looked over at Kenny, and Milo than at Richard in one swift move of the head all of them headed towards the slide door.

That's him Tonya yelled That's him.

Him who? Richard asked putting his hand up to his mouth him who?

Richard Tonya yell how? Why? Where did you meet him?

Who? What are you talking about?

Richard that man the one that was just behind you He is the man that tried to kill me.

Richard was in shock.

Christina came over to where Richard and Tonya was standing what happen to the guys?

Milo ran after Samuel and Mylz, and Kenny was not far behind.

Call the police Kenny shouted.

What happen? Christina said, as Tonya dialed 911.

There chasing the guy who tried to kill me.

What where was he at? Christina asked.

Richard did you see this guy she said.

Its Samuel he said to Christina.

What?

This is 911 what is your emergency she heard the voice say.

We need the police over at 12378 west 5th Ave.

What is going on?

We have a murder running down the street and my boyfriend and my friends are chasing him please get over here.

I have a car on the way, said the lady on the phone.

Catch his ass Milo said to Kenny.

This dude is running like he has rockets on his shoes Kenny yelled back as he saw Samuel jump over the fence.

Ill go the other way,

Mylz yelled as he cut through the yard to his right.

All of them ran through the neighbor hood for about an hour before they decided to return to the house where the police was standing talking to Christina and Tonya.

Look their they are Tonya said did you guy's get him?

No. His ass was running for his life Kenny said.

That mutherfucker musta had rockets on his shoes.

He was hitting fences like a pro Milo said.

I have five cars in the area and more on the way we'll catch him. Officer Johnson replied

I hope so that was him I know it was him the first time I saw that face.

Tonya turned around real fast where is Richard? she said in a harsh way.

Christina Looked around the front yard and did not see him.

I think he's inside with an officer.

He was dating a mad man what is going on.

He didn't know Christina said with consideration for her friend he is just as much a victim as you are.

No one ever saw this guy but you and his other victims.

Yeah I guess your right Tonya said, let's go find Richard.

We have him in custody Milo heard a voice say through the officer radio.

Officer Johnson pushed the button on his mike and gave a big 10 4.

We have him he said to Mylz and Milo. Can you bring the girls back out of the house so we can go to the location and see if it's the right person.

Milo went into the house to get Tonya, Hey sis I think they found this motherfucker.

The officer wants you to go with him to see if it's him, come on.

The Dj was still rocking and the party was jumping, Richard and Christina stood in his room up stairs in shock, I can't believe what just happen Richard said softly.

Its ok Christina told him I think this happen for a reason this man might have hurt another woman.

Tonya arrived with the officer to see Samuel standing in front of a police car with hand cuffs on.

That's him she said as she tried to get out the back of the police car.

No no you can't go over there the officer said.

I just want to get a better look she said in a voice that did not sit well with the officer.

He did not know what had happen to Tonya but he could tell that she was pissed.

Milo had followed the police to the location he had already gotten out of his car and blended in with the crowed.

Waiting for a chance to get close to the guy, Just as another cop call the officer that was standing by the car with Samuel over to speak to him Milo saw his opportunity.

Milo ran up and hit Samuel so hard that he was out on the ground bleeding from the face.

Hold it right there he heard the officers say, He looked back and about three officers had their gun's drawn and pointed at him.

Get this motherfucker out of here he yelled are you will be shooting me tonight.

No Tonya yelled as she took off running towards her brother.

Get back she heard the officers yell get back.

Tonya kept running until she was standing blocking Milo.

Detective Dent had just arrived on the scene as thing was about to get totally out of control.

By now the crowed had started getting wild the people wanted a piece of this murder.

Put your guns away Detective Dent hollered put them away. He walked over to Tonya and Milo Come on you guys we have him let the officers do their job.

Tonya hugged Milo and cryied.

The officers picked up Samuel, put him in the car in a hurry and drove away.

At the station, Samuel was book in and finger printed, to the surprise of the police, he has over ten aliases in three states.

This guy has been busy after running a full back ground on him it was found out that he was an only child of a well known Real Estate agent who sold only Million dollar homes.

She was murdered about three years ago and it is still an open case, her murder has never been found.

Detective Dent went into the room where Samuel was waiting he introduced himself and sat down.

What do you people want?

You will find out soon enough Detective Dent said.

Before you say a word to me man I want to call my lawyer.

That ended the interview right there Detective Dent replied.

Tonya and Milo, Christina, Kenny and Mylz returned to Tonya house to just calm down.

Milo we can't tell mom and dad about this until we here from Detective dent you here me?

Who wants a drink Christina asked.

I'll take one every one said at once, man I haven't sprinted like that in a long time Kenny said with a smirk on his lips.

You guys took off so fast after that guy is seem like the house was on fire.

Back at Richard's house did you guys think I was tripping Tonya asked.

I thought you had one drink two many Christina said but I know that you had only one so you had to have seen some one.

I thought you were tripping sis Milo said.

I didn't know what to think Mylz said smiling, No one saw this guy but you.

I will never forget his face either Tonya said I will never forget him and as soon as I get a chance I'm going to kick his ass across that court room, you can bet on that.

We will all be there with you.

I hope so because it will take all of you and Jesus to keep me off his ass.

I hope he don't get one of those fancy lawyers to give him a change of venue.

Than everyone eyes turned, looked over at Kenny.

What, Kenny said holding up both hands I'm not taking the case and no one in my firm better not either.

Kenny went to the office that Monday to find out he had received a call from Samuel wanting to hire him to represent him.

Kenny's assistant stuck her head in his office and asked did you get that message that I placed in your in box?

Hey good morning, yes I did but this case I want nothing to do with and no one in this company will be taking this case either.

Wow! What are you talking about Kenny?

This is the man, who tried to murder Tonya and the person responsible for the other Realtors murders.

Are you sure?

Yes I was there Saturday night when he got arrested.

What?

It's a long story, I really don't know what this dude real name is.

We are not getting involved in this case at all.

Ok if you say so.

Ring Ring

Hello.

Hey sweetheart Mylz said.

Hello; are you at work?

Yes its very busy I was just thinking about you.

Well I just got home from the gym and now I'm heading for the bath.

I wish I could join you Mylz teasingly said.

Come on you. Tonya said softly.

What, about later?

Sure, what time will you be off? Tonya asked.

I think about 7 or 8 is that good for you?

Sounds great I'll have something cooked so you want run out of energy again.

What are you talking about Mylz ask laughing.

The other night you know I unleashed on your ass and you were so out of energy.

I think you said you didn't get any sleep that day or something like that Tonya laughed.

Well young lady, that want happen tonight Ill be ready to eat dinner and you.

That sounds great, sweetheart Tonya felt heat raising in her body.

I'm getting hot already so you better get back to work before you start something on this phone.

You know Dr. your something special.

I want to let you know that I can't be duplicated either.

I feel that you are my Miss right and I'll be your Mr. right.

I want you to be my Mr. right now; but I'll hold off until you get off work Tonya said in a playful way. It's my duty to make you woozie Tonya said with a little giggle.

Oh you got jokes, I hope you can back up all that big talk.

Unleash what you got than.

I want you to sink it in like a Tiger Woods putt.

Girl your on a roll but I'll have you thinking I created sex keep it up.

Ok we will stop now go back to work and I will see you when you get here.

Smiling they both hang up.

Christina was working late today her and Kenny spent a weekend away from the nuisance of the past few days.

Kenny was working hard at the office looking for way to keep this murder off of the street.

This is a very dangerous man and it will take every thing you have to keep this guy in jail Kenny explain to his associates that he has working on this investigation part.

We all need to contribute all of the information we find to the District Attorney so he builds a strong case on this guy.

It's getting late everyone so let's call it a night and I'll see you all in the morning bright and early.

Kenny left his boardroom and headed for his office.

Hey Girl Tonya answer her phone, what's up?

How are you doing Christina said?

Man all is well I'm waiting for Mr. right as he call himself.

Who?

Mylz he said he is my Mr. right, I told him I want him to be my Mr. right now.

Your ass is crazy Christing laughed.

How's work? Are you still at the office?

Yes about to leave get myself home and sit in the tub.

Hey, how was the trip? Tonya asked

Shit it was the bomb we walked, talked, relaxed and just enjoyed each other's company.

San Francisco was a little cold.

It's always cold in the bay area Tonya said.

Kenny was just great he tried to put it down.

That man was serious about pleasing me and you know that I was not about to let him out do me.

I made his soul blush, he thought he was a adolescent all over again.

I tell you what I'll meet you at the gym in the morning and you finish telling me about your trip

Ok Christina said in a very tired voice ill see you at seven.

The gym was cracking all of the regular morning crew was there saying hello to each other and working hard on there bodies.

Christina and I always start with a ten-minute warm up on the treadmill.

So finish the story.

Girl Kenny not only tried to put it on me but he also gave me this Christina said as she held up her left hand.

Tonya and Christina screamed everyone in the cardio section turn to see what was wrong.

That is so big Tonya said.

I know, I was so shocked.

He just . . . .

Girl sit, tell me the whole story, how, what did he say.

Slow down Christina said, let's go walk the track because I know that everyone on the treadmill will be trying to listen.

That is a big beautiful ring.

Wow!!! I'm so excited for you Tonya said.

Girl calm down it was very nice how he did it.

We had dinner the first night we arrived at pier 59 and we talk about all of the things that had happened you know over these last few months.

How life is to short and how none of us is promised tomorrow.

Yeah Tonya said really.

He was just a little serious so I asked if everything was all right.

I thought he was going to maybe, say we need a little time away from each other.

Girl, why would you think that?

I'm not sure I just had not seen that side of Kenny plus he was the one who wanted to leave town and get away from everyone.

Anyway we had a very serious talk and he asked me what plans did I have for my future and how did I feel about this relationship we were having.

Than I really began to feel funny, where was all this going I thought.

You were tripping Tonya replied, you know that he is in love with you.

Ray Charles can see that.

Christina laughed.

It was just, we never talked about our future we took one day at a time and that felt good.

Bullshit, you know you want that man's last name.

Christina held up her ring and smiled.

So the next day after a long work out that night I woke up to breakfast in bed and a beautiful gold box sitting on my plate with my fine ass man on his knee by the side of the bed looking me straight in my eyes and he asked me to marry him.

And than Tonya asked with excited.

Tears ran down my face I was so nervous I shook as I grab him saying yes' yes I will marry you.

Kenny was just thrilled.

Tonight we are meeting with our families to let them know, but I had to tell you.

Christina said but you can't tell Mylz you all are coming to my house for dinner tonight.

Ok I don't know nothing Tonya said smiling.

Pinky swear Christina said holding up her right pinky.

Call Mylz right now and let him know that we have planed dinner for everyone tonight.

Tonight was going to be a great night Tonya thought to her self her best friend had just got engaged that made her feel good.

They worked out for an hour and a half and then shower and dressed for worked see you tonight Christina said as she drove off heading to her office.

As Tonya headed to her office she though how her and Christina had always said that they would have a double wedding.

This was there dream ever since the fifth grade.

Christina pulled up in the parking spot right next to Mylz Black BMW

Hey, Dr.

Hi Christina is every thing ready for tonight he asked.

Yes, she saw my ring and she don't have a clue.

I spoke with her mom, dad, and brother Mylz they will all be there tonight.

Perfect Christina said I'll have everything ready about seven.

Tonya and Mylz meet at her house about six and had a few minutes to relax while talking about there eventful day.

Mylz was watching the clock he was excited about tonight.

It's time to go sweetheart didn't she say that dinner starts at seven?

Yes I know just let me get my jacket.

Mylz smiled as he walked towards Tonya to help her with her jacket.

Thanks, you must be hungry babe it seems like your in a rush.

No, I'm ok you know I don't want to be late you know that Christina parents will be there.

Babe, What is this dinner about Mylz ask smiling.

I not telling, you will see when you get there.

I hope it's good news not bad.

I think Christina have good news she was really happy this morning at the gym.

O Yeah, what about? Mylz ask as he turned to see if Tonya would tell him what he already knew.

You will here the news just like everyone else, so just get there.

Yes, mom Christina yelled from the kitchen, They will be here on time.

Pops and Kenney sat in the living room watching the Lakers play along with Tonya parents.

Call the foul pops yelled as he stood up, man are they kidding me did you see how he knocked

Koby to the ground?

That's cold Kenny said the ref should have called that.

All right, All right get him Koby take the ball pops yelled now shot.... Oyeah all net

See that's why they be trying to hurt the boy pops said smiling.

Kenny had arrived about 30 minutes ago and took a seat in the living room with pops to check out the game.

The house was filling up with all the expected guest and thing were going just as planed.

Tonya and Mylz just arrived as the dinner was just being removed from the oven

Hey all Tonya said as she let her self in.

Hi Tony every one said Hi Mylz they all said as he made his way to the living room to sit and see the last part of the game.

What's the score he asked.

Man pops said you missed a cold blow they tried to hurt my boy Koby.

What?

Yeah man that other cat in number 45 just knocked Koby down so hard that my boy had to grab his elbow and rub it he hit the ground hard.

Man Kenny yelled and the ref did nothing.

I missed all the excitement Mylz said.

Ok men Mrs. Gardner said it's dinner time come get it while its hot.

Baby the game is almost done give us a pass for five minutes please pops asked softly.

Well it's on the table and we will be in there waiting.

Let me look at that ring one more time Tonya asked Christina.

Covering her mouth Tonya made a little scream.

Your so crazy Christina said.

I wish Tonya said I hope the best for you girl.

You will have your turn next I know it Christina replied.

Tonya looked over at the living room, and saw Mylz looking at her, she smiled.

Well, Im starving, I didn't have a bit because I knew that it would be a soul food feast here to night.

By the looks of it I was right Tonya said.

The dinner was great talk at dinner went smooth we all laugh, and enjoyed the meal and now it was time for Tonya favorite desert.

Mom came out of the kitchen with a great big pan of peach cobbler and vanilla ice cream.

Mylz stood up and said that he had an announcement to make.

To the Gardners and Williams thanks for hosting such a great dinner the food was great and to Kenny and Christina congrat's on your engagement.

Tonya will you stand please he asked softly.

Tonya looked up at him with a surprise look on her face she did not have any thing to say she already know about the engagement she thought to herself.

Everyone was looking so serious she thought.

I just want to eat my peach cobbler and ice cream

What the hell: is next no bad news she thought.

Mylz look deep in her eyes, I love you and I know you thought that this dinner was for Christina.

I gathered every one together so I can ask you my love to marry me.

Tonya stood there looking very shock and surprise to here what Mylz had just asked.

Looking over at everyone at the table to seeing the great big smiles on their faces she knew that it was real.

Mylz stood there for what seems like an hour waiting for his answer.

Tears ran down Tonya face Tears of joy and excitement Yes, Yes she said as she turned to see the five carrot diamond ring set in a white gold setting in a beautiful gold ring box.

Christina smiled told Tonya all that she wanted to know she knew all the time.

Their dreams would come true a double wedding.

Claps filled the room as Tonya and Mylz kissed.